INSTRUMENT OF REVENGE

Anne Stewart was in the same manor house as her husband, Viscount Merrick, for the first time in many months. Not that he was here of his own free will. Only an official family reunion of the Merrick clan could have forced him to reluctantly leave his London mistress to see again the wife he had so willingly left.

Now at last Anne had her chance to strike back at him.

She even had a weapon very close at hand.

A most attractive and extremely dangerous weapon named Jack Frazier—who would let her use him only if she let him use her. . . .

(For a list of other Signet Regency Romances by Mary Balogh, please turn page. . . .)

THE FIRST
SNOWDROP

MARY BALOGH

A SIGNET BOOK

SIGNET
Published by the Penguin Group
Penguin Books USA Inc., 375 Hudson Street,
New York, New York 10014, U.S.A.
Penguin Books Ltd, 27 Wrights Lane,
London W8 5TZ, England
Penguin Books Australia Ltd, Ringwood,
Victoria, Australia
Penguin Books Canada Ltd, 10 Alcorn Avenue,
Toronto, Ontario, Canada M4V 3B2
Penguin Books (N.Z.) Ltd, 182–190 Wairau Road,
Auckland 10, New Zealand

Penguin Books Ltd, Registered Offices:
Harmondsworth, Middlesex, England

Published by Signet, an imprint of Dutton Signet,
a division of Penguin Books USA Inc.

First Printing, September, 1986
11 10 9 8 7 6 5 4 3

 REGISTERED TRADEMARK—MARCA REGISTRADA

Printed in the United States of America

PART ONE

December, 1814

1 It was not a dark night. It was as light as the traveler had hoped it would be. He could see the road ahead of him clearly enough that he kept his horse to its steady canter without fear that it would lose its way or stumble into one of the many ruts and potholes on the road's surface, laming itself and throwing its rider. In fact, with a tightening of his knees on the horse's flanks, he urged it to a slightly faster pace yet. He still hoped to reach the next sizable town before stopping for the night, and that must be close to fifteen miles distant. Time was in his favor; it was still only early evening despite the darkness. Night fell early in December.

It was as he had hoped, but Alexander Stewart, Viscount Merrick, nevertheless felt uneasy. It was moonlight and starlight that he had bargained on to light his way, not these heavy, low clouds that appeared a leaden gray color and illumined the landscape despite the time of evening. The light was eerie, certainly not like daylight, but not natural for nighttime, either. Those were snow clouds, if ever he had seen any, and they were about to loose their load. The air had become warmer during the past hour, not colder as one might expect with the falling of darkness. The breeze that had chilled his left cheek for most of the afternoon had died completely away.

Damn! He was going to be forced to stop more than ten miles sooner than he had planned, and doubtless at a country inn where the bedsheets would be un-aired, the food less than appetizing, and the service uncouth. From the look of those clouds, he judged that he might even consider himself fortunate if he could leave the inn tomorrow morning. He pulled his beaver hat further forward on his head as the first large snowflake landed on the back of his leather glove, and rode grimly on.

He should have listened to Horace that morning, much as he hated to admit his error. His friend had warned him that the weather was about to take a turn for the worse.

"Take m' word for it," Horace Reed had said, folding his hands across his large stomach and nod-ding his head against his chest so that his two chins doubled in number. "I always know when bad weath-er's on the way. M' feet swell and m' legs ache and I lose m' appetite." He had patted his mouth with a linen napkin and thrown it down onto his empty breakfast plate.

Merrick had grinned. "Was it three eggs or two you ate with your sausage and bacon and kidneys?" he had asked innocently.

Horace's chins had returned to normality as he raised his head. "Laugh if you like, Alex," he had admonished his skeptical friend, "but it will surely rain before the day is out. Or snow, more likely, at this time of year. You'd better stay another day or two, old boy. Better here than in some country inn, where you won't get a decent feed or a comfortable fire."

But Merrick had resisted. Even if he had had faith in his friend's unorthodox manner of forecasting the weather, he probably would have held to his plans, he reflected now. He pulled up the collar of his greatcoat and huddled down inside it until the gar-

ment threatened to push his beaver from his head.
Old Horace had been a close friend since their university days, when he had attached himself to the
more attractive and charismatic viscount with a loyalty bordering on hero-worship. Not that it had been
a one-sided friendship. Horace had been an intelligent and sensible student who helped Merrick de-
velop his own mind and ideas. And they had remained
friends. When news that Reed's father had died suddenly reached Merrick in London, he had ridden
the two-day journey with the sole purpose of offering comfort and support.

But two weeks had been long enough. Too long!
He had to get back, could not imagine, in fact, why
he had been contented to be away so long. He was
finally very close to getting his life in order. He now
found that he could bear to wait no longer to complete the process. And so he had insisted on leaving.

Now, after all, it began to look as if he might not
reach London tomorrow but be forced to put up
along the way. The wind had risen, not the quicken-
ing breeze of the afternoon, but a strong and cutting
force that blew directly into his face and stung his
eyes. Snow was falling heavily, large white flakes that
stayed where they landed and did not immediately
melt. The eerie light still held, but it no longer served
his purpose. The wind alone would have made him
squint. The snow, slanting constantly across his line
of vision, threatened to mesmerize him and made it
impossible for him to see more than a few feet ahead.

Merrick cursed aloud and noticed, by looking down
at his horse's hooves, that there was already a thin
covering of snow on the road. If it continued to fall
at this rate—and there was every indication that it
would do so—it would soon be difficult to distinguish between the surface of the road and the fields
that stretched to either side. He peered intently ahead
and to both sides, trying to distinguish any light that
might signal a habitation. He would have to settle for
any shelter he could find, even a laborer's cottage. A

country inn might be beyond his reach. He shrugged up his shoulders again in the hope that his ears would share some of the warmth of his coat. He was very thankful for the twelve heavy capes of his fashionable greatcoat, which Horace had laughed at only two weeks before, claiming that he would have stooped shoulders before he reached his middle years if he persisted in wearing such a garment.

Merrick wondered if it was snowing in London, too. Would Lorraine be going out tonight—to some party, or to the theater, perhaps? He hoped she would be safe, then smiled at his own absurdity. With parents who doted on her, an abigail who would have breathed for her mistress if by doing so she might save the young lady some effort, and a coachman who prided himself on avoiding every bump and crack in the streets that his mistress might not be jolted unnecessarily, he did not believe he need worry. If she did venture out, she would be wrapped in furs and her safety put above all other considerations.

When he finally returned, they would at last make a formal announcement of their betrothal. No sooner than her eighteenth birthday, her papa, the Marquess of Hadley, had said. And she would be eighteen in three days' time. It had seemed a long wait. He had known almost as soon as he met her during the previous Season that he wanted her as his wife, but she had been very young. Merrick had never understood why her father had allowed her to make her come-out if he considered her not old enough to be betrothed. After all, bringing out a daughter was synonymous with announcing to the *ton* that one was seeking a husband for her. However, he had to feel thankful that his courtship had proceeded as smoothly as it had. Lorraine had liked him from the start, as had her mother. And Hadley had made no objection to the match beyond the short delay. He had allowed Merrick to visit his daughter and to be her frequent escort.

Merrick still found it hard to believe that he was

actually welcoming the thought of marriage. It had been the last thing on his mind even a year ago. He was young—a mere seven-and-twenty even now—and wealthy and attractive, he knew. He had borne his title from infancy, when his parents had died, and was heir to a dukedom and another fortune. Ever since coming down from university, he had been bent on enjoying life to the full—traveling, socializing, participating in all strenuous sports, womanizing. His grandmother, the Duchess of Portland, had frequently hinted that it would soon be time to think of settling down, but he had always laughed and kissed her lightly on the forehead, declaring that she would not so easily wind him around her little finger as she did his grandfather. That comment could always be counted upon to make her loudly argumentative. And he was invariably an "impudent puppy." But she would forget about the topic that had provoked his impudence.

Earlier that year, though, she had been more persistent, declaring that she had found him just the girl for his future duchess. Merrick had grinned good-naturedly as she had described this paragon of beauty and virtue, who would be attending her ball the following week. He could not avoid the introduction, as he was honor-bound to attend the ball himself. But to his own surprise, he had discovered that he had no wish to escape the ordeal. The girl was a beauty, tall with a willowy slimness, masses of blond curls framing an oval face, and china-blue eyes that looked on the world with a strange combination of innocence and self-assurance.

Merrick had soon concluded that, since he must settle down sooner or later, it might as well be sooner. It would be a good match. The girl was highborn and well-trained in the kind of life she would have to lead as his wife. Young as she was, she knew how to manage a household and how to inspire loyalty, even adoration, in subordinates. She had the kind of poise that would carry her through the formal state

occasions that they must face when he succeeded to
the dukedom—which, please heaven, would not be
too soon. And even though he had made the decision with his head, Merrick had to admit that the
more personal aspect of the marriage was far from
distasteful to his mind. He frequently let his eyes
roam over her young, untouched body and looked
forward with some impatience to the time when he
would have the right to explore with his hands rather
than his eyes. He had not yet touched her, of course.
She had not let him kiss more than her hand, and
even that only once when she had consented to become betrothed to him as soon as her birthday came.
In the meantime, he soothed his frustrations with
other female companions.

He wanted very much to see her again. Two weeks
had seemed an eternity. Unconsciously, he urged his
horse on, only to ease back firmly on the reins as he
felt one hoof slip on the snow. He cursed again and
passed one gloved hand across his eyes in a vain
effort to shake off the glare that made them ache
with a sharp pain. He would be lucky to find anywhere to spend the night. He would probably be
found dead of exposure a week or so from now
when the snow finally melted, he thought wryly. He
slid reluctantly from his horse's back and took a firm
hold of the reins close to the bit. He could not risk
either his horse's or his own safety any longer by
riding.

The snow was disconcertingly deep. His boots sank
immediately above the ankles. As he waded on, he
was soon in almost to his knees. It was impossible to
tell where the road was or in which direction he
walked. What a fool he had been! Even if old Horace's reasoning that morning had been somewhat
unbelievable, the evidence of his own senses as the
afternoon progressed should have been enough. He
had seen those clouds gathering, had recognized the
signs. He had passed through two villages after realizing that a storm was on the way. But he had re-

fused to acknowledge the message of his own brain.
And here he was, a prize idiot, in the middle of
nowhere, becoming increasingly aware of the real
danger of his situation.

At the moment when he admitted this final thought,
he jerked his eyes back to the spot that they had just
passed. Had he really seen a light, or was his anxiety
causing him hallucinations? He held on to the reins
with an iron hand as his horse snorted and tried to
toss its head in protest against the irritation of the
snow. He narrowed his eyes and gazed intently. He
sagged with relief when the light once again appeared through the driving snow, small but steady.
A house. It must come from a house.

Merrick turned in its direction, pulling the horse
firmly along with him. He dared not take his eyes
from the faint light, willed it to stay alight, prayed
that the inhabitants would not decide to snuff the
candles and go to bed. He stumbled frequently and
sometimes sank above his knees into a windblown
drift. But the light held steady and gradually took
form as that thrown by a branch of candles inside a
square window. It came from a fairly large and imposing brick house, Merrick realized as the walls
loomed out of the almost blinding curtain of snow.
He was not, after all, going to have to demand hospitality from some cottager. Not that he would really
care at the moment. He was chilled to the bone and
had received a bad scare. Any hovel would have
seemed like a glimpse of heaven.

He stumbled to the front door, abandoning his
hold on his horse's reins only in order to stagger up
the steps that led up to it, their true contours completely masked by the heavy fall of snow. He grasped
the iron knocker and banged it against the door. It
seemed to him an age until he heard bolts being
drawn back at the other side of the door. He had
banged three times.

The door was swung back as quickly as such a
heavy portal could be opened by a small female.

"Oh, Bruce," she was saying even before she could see who was waiting so impatiently to be let in, "you really should not have . . . Oh!" A hand went to her throat when she saw that it was not Bruce, whoever he might be.

"Let me in, my good girl," Merrick said firmly, shouldering his way past her into the hallway. "I shall need to beg hospitality. But first, is there someone who can stable my horse and perhaps brush him down for me?"

"Oh, no," she said hesitantly, "there is no one, sir."

He turned impatiently. "No one willing to brave a storm for the sake of a horse?" he asked coldly.

"No," she said anxiously. "There are no servants here, sir. Is your horse outside?"

"Do you see it in the hallway?" he asked sharply, then gave himself a mental shake as he pulled his leather gloves free of fingers that were already beginning to tingle with returning warmth. He was not usually abrupt with servants. "Announce me, please. Then I shall stable the horse myself."

The girl hesitated, so that again he swung in her direction and looked full at her for the first time. Small, plain, mousy, overplump, drably dressed, overanxious. He raised his eyebrows.

"There is no one here," she said, "except me, sir."

Merrick continued to stare. "Everyone is out and has left the house in the care of one girl?" he asked incredulously.

"Bruce—my brother—is supposed to be back," she explained, "but the storm will surely keep him in town." Her look of anxiety deepened into one of near fright as she appeared to realize how much of her own vulnerability she had revealed.

"Well," he said matter-of-factly, his eyes coolly sweeping her figure once more, "we shall have to manage as best we can, my girl. I shall begin by seeing to my horse if you would give me the direction to the stables. I would be much obliged to you if you will have brandy and some food available to me when I return. Some bread or cold meat or whatever you have. I will not expect a feast. And see that the fires are well built up."

She stared back at him, cheeks stained with color. "Yes, sir," she said. "The stables are west of the house. You would see them clearly if it were not for the snow."

Merrick pulled his gloves back on and strode back to the door, bracing himself to face the cold and the storm again. His horse had not moved, but stood snorting and pawing at the ground as if by so doing it might disperse the nuisance that was attacking it from all directions. The stables were close to the house, Merrick discovered with some relief. Only one of the many stalls was occupied, but he found straw and water, a brush with which to care for his own animal, and a blanket with which to cover it. He felt the warmth creeping back into his own limbs as he worked.

The family must be away from home and had left a skeleton staff. Very much a skeleton staff. It appeared that this girl and her brother ran the household alone. It must be quite a formidable task even if there was no family to tend to. That Bruce fellow must be a careless kind of servant to leave house and sister alone while he, no doubt, was roistering in a nearby village, probably amusing himself with the village ale and the village wenches. However, he must be eternally grateful that the man had not taken his sister with him. He would still be wading around the countryside if he had not seen her light.

When Merrick returned to the house, carrying the small leather bag that contained all he had considered essential for the journey, the girl was there in the hallway again, looking just as uneasy as when he had left her. Her hands were twisting the sides of her singularly unattractive gray wool dress. Anxious gray eyes watched him from beneath the frill of a cotton cap.

"I have built up the fire in the library, sir," she

said. "That is the warmest room. The brandy is on the side table. I am heating some soup for you. It will not be long, I believe."

"Thank you," he said, putting down his bag on the floor, removing his gloves and his beaver hat and handing them to her. "That all sounds quite satisfactory." He removed his greatcoat and flung it down onto a chair in the hallway. The girl still held his hat and gloves. She appeared uncertain what to do with them. Merrick rubbed his hands together briskly. "Bring the food as soon as it is ready," he said. "What is your name, girl?"

The color was back in her cheeks again. "Anne," she said. "Anne Parrish, sir."

He nodded. "Merrick," he said. "Viscount Merrick." And he turned toward the library, which she had indicated earlier, strode inside, and shut the door behind him.

When the girl entered the room ten minutes later, without knocking, and placed a tray loaded with soup, bread, and cake, on the table beside him, Merrick had already taken possession of a worn but comfortably upholstered chair close to the roaring log fire. His booted feet, crossed at the ankles, were stretched across the hearth. A glass, half-filled with brandy, was cupped in his palm, the stem passing between his middle and forefingers. He was reveling in the glory of feeling warm inside and out. He was even feeling pleasantly drowsy.

He smiled at the girl as she set down the tray and straightened up. "Thank you, Anne," he said. "You have saved my life tonight."

"It is not much, my lord," she said anxiously, indicating the tray. "But it would take a long time to make a proper meal for you."

"If you only knew how good it looks to me, under the circumstances, my girl, you would make no apology," Merrick said, continuing to smile warmly at her.

The girl made no move to leave but continued to

stand beside the table, her hands clasped in front of her. She was looking at him, flushing. So it was like that, was it? Merrick's smile turned to one of amusement.

"Sit down, Anne," he said. "You may eat the cake. I am sure I will have no room left for it by the time I have eaten this bread. It is quite excellent. Did you make it?"

"Oh, no," she replied. "No, my lord."

She sat in the chair across from him, on the very edge of the seat, her hands still clasped stiffly in her lap. She continued to gaze at him in the anxious way that more and more amused him.

Merrick's eyes narrowed lazily as he examined her from head to toe. Poor girl, she did not have much to recommend her. The plump figure and the too-round face gave her an almost childish appearance. It was no wonder the brother had not taken her with him to town. She was probably not a wench much in demand. However, she clearly was not a child. She knew how to send out an open-enough invitation.

"Is the town you talked of far away, Anne?" he asked.

"All of three miles, my lord," she said, "an almost impossible distance on a night like this." And she blushed painfully again and looked almost frightened for a moment.

"You must not worry about Bruce," Merrick said, smiling across at her. He leaned back from the tray, which was now empty of all except the plate of cake, and took up the brandy glass again. He swirled the contents absently in his hand. "He would not even attempt the distance on a night like this. And you have me to protect you." His eyes laughed at her.

Her hands were pleating and twisting the dress in her lap. She stared across at him and said nothing. His eyes continued to laugh. Why not? he was thinking. It was going to be a long and chilly night and the girl at least looked clean. It would be a shame to reject such a generous offer. And the poor girl could not have many thrills in her life. Why not?

"Will you show me my room, Anne?" he asked quietly, not removing his eyes from hers. "Is there one made up?"

"Yes, my lord," she said quickly, jumping to her feet. "You must have the master bedroom. It is the only one I am sure is aired. And there is a fire there."

Merrick's eyebrows rose. "Indeed?" he said. "Then lead the way, girl."

She took the branched candlestick from the mantel and hurried to the door. Merrick followed, the brandy glass still dangling from his fingers. He picked up his bag in the hallway and amused himself with an examination of the back view of the maid as she preceded him up the wooden staircase and along a short passageway until she stopped and opened a door. She disappeared inside and was setting the candles on a dresser when he entered. She turned toward him.

"I believe you will have everything you need here, my lord," she said, and she blushed yet again. "If you wish, you may use a nightshirt from this drawer." She indicated one in another dresser.

"I do not believe I shall have need of one," Merrick said, his eyes laughing at her again. "Will you turn the bedclothes down for me, Anne?"

She hesitated, but she crossed to the high bed and bent over it as she folded back the blankets and the top sheet.

Merrick came up behind her and waited for her movements to stop as she became aware of his closeness. He passed an arm in front of her and let his hand trail back toward him across her breasts. They were full and firm. Not bad at all, in fact.

She did nothing for a moment, though he heard a ragged intake of breath. Then she turned toward him, her eyes wide, her cheeks deeply flushed. He

smiled knowingly down at her. Her lips, too, were
not unpleasant beneath his own. They were warm
and soft. He tried to gain entrance to her mouth by
running his tongue lightly back and forth across her
lips and finally stabbing between them, but he en-
countered only her teeth firmly clamped together.
She whimpered a little against his mouth when he
put a hand behind her hips and brought her against
him. She was stiff and unyielding.

Hell and damnation, he thought suddenly, she was
not a virgin, was she? One naturally assumed that
even the most unattractive of maids had had some
small share of rolls in the hay. This girl acted as if she
had no idea of what he was about, though she offered no active resistance. He lifted his head and
held her loosely by the waist.

"Have you not been touched before, Anne?" he
asked.

"My lord?" she said, her eyes bewildered.

"Have you had no man inside you, girl?" he asked.

Her mouth moved but no sound came out. She
had lost all control of her facial muscles and began
to tremble jerkily against his hands.

"Don't be frightened," he said gently. "I am not
going to ravish you, Anne. You were willing, I believe, but now find that the act takes more courage
than you presently possess. Go to bed, girl. You are
in no danger from me." He kissed her lightly on the
forehead.

She stared at him for a moment until he smiled,
stepped aside, and gestured mockingly with one hand
toward the door. She fled finally in ungainly haste,
neglecting to take a candle with her.

Merrick gazed at the bed and shrugged. Why had
he suddenly displayed that pointless gallantry? She
had smelled good, of some unidentified soap. She
would not have stopped him. She would certainly
have helped warm the bed on a night like this. But,
of course, there would have been the tears, and
perhaps hysterics, afterward. And such an innocent

would probably have allowed him to get her with child. He supposed it really was not entirely fair that servants be expected to bear such shame just because they were servants. He shrugged again, eyed with misgiving those cold-looking silk sheets, and gazed first at the dying fire in the fireplace and then at the drawer that, with any luck, would contain some warm nightshirts.

2 The time had come when Bruce Parrish had been forced to admit defeat. For three years he had struggled to retain the land he still held and somehow to make it pay its way. He had worked and economized in order to keep the house and the gardens neat and in order. But it was a sad fact that sometimes the sins of the fathers are visited upon the children.

The Honorable Jonathon Parrish, younger son of a baron, had been left in comfortable circumstances on the death of his mother. There had been a sizable estate and an impressive, if not imposing, house. He should have been able to live comfortably on the income from his land and rents, especially since his wife had presented him with only two children. But the man never accepted the fact that it was his elder brother, less intelligent and with less charm and good looks than he, who had inherited the title and the paternal home. Jonathon Parrish had taken little interest in his property, using it only as a source of income to finance his hunting and his card-playing and his hard drinking.

When he died, his son, Bruce, far different in character from himself, discovered that his father's debts were enormous and that the land had been

neglected for years. He already knew that the house
furnishings had been allowed to grow shabby and
the once-landscaped gardens overgrown. Bruce Parrish had tried, had puzzled over the problems for
three years. But finally he had been forced to admit
that he would never be able to both pay back his
father's debts and spend the money necessary to
recover the fortunes of the estate. He was a serious
young man whose sense of duty was overdeveloped.
If he must make a choice, he would have to choose
repaying the debtors, who had already waited far too
long. He decided that the house and the land must
be leased. Not sold. He could not bear the thought
of that—not yet, anyway. He would try what he
could do with the lease money and what he could
earn.

Bruce Parrish had a sister five years his junior.
She had acted as their father's housekeeper and as
his own for so long that he took her presence very
much for granted. He never considered consulting
her on any of the many problems that beset him.
This occasion was no exception. He must be gain-
fully employed; she must come with him and keep
his house, even though it was to be a far humbler
abode than the one they had always known. She was
informed only one week before they were to remove
themselves from their childhood home that he was
to be employed as a schoolmaster in a town thirty
miles distant and that she was to go with him to live
in the small brick schoolhouse that adjoined the school.

Anne Parrish did not put up any fight. She had
always been a quiet girl, one who was inclined to be
disregarded by those with whom she lived closely.
But she observed with a keen intelligence all that
happened around her. She had understood what
ruin her father's way of life was bringing to his
family. She had watched her brother's efforts to re-
verse the process of years and had seen that it was
hopeless. She knew that his decision was the only
one that could have been made.

And, truth to tell, Anne did not feel that she would be losing a great deal. She had not been happy for four years, since she had been eighteen. Home had never been a pleasant place for her since the death of her mother eight years before. Her father had been almost always in his cups, always involved in his own selfish activities. His cronies had frequently haunted the house, their presence a trial enough even before Anne had reached the age to attract their coarse gallantry. Afterward it had been almost unendurable. Her father, when he noticed her at all, treated her as if she were a servant, and greeted with loud amusement any sign he saw of one of his drinking companions pinching her or even stealing a kiss.

Bruce might have made her life more tolerable. He certainly had none of their father's vices and coldly drove from the premises one man whom he caught addressing her as "my lovely." But unfortunately, he went to the opposite extreme. He was harsh and humorless. He viewed as sinful anything that suggested enjoyment or the slightest frivolity. He disapproved vocally of the only two people of whom Anne had ever been truly fond since her mother's death.

Sonia Davies was the only daughter of a neighboring landowner, an extremely pretty and vivacious young lady. She and Anne were almost of an age. They had always been close friends. And, indeed, Bruce had always appeared to like the girl until she grew to a very attractive womanhood. From that time on, he had voiced nothing but criticism of her preoccupation with her looks and with fashion and of her obvious enjoyment of gaiety. Anne had never considered herself very pretty, especially in comparison with her friend, but she had been satisfied with herself, had enjoyed poring over fashion plates with Sonia, had loved the afternoons they often spent together experimenting with each other's hair, planning their futures, the type of men they would marry, the number of children they would have. Sonia had left more than four years before for a London Season and had married a man with a comfortable income and a home sixty miles distant. Anne had seen her only twice since, though they corresponded regularly.

Then there had been Dennis Poole. He also had been a neighbor, a cousin of Sonia's, in fact. Anne had loved him for as long back as she could remember. Red-haired, brown-eyed, and extremely tall as he grew to manhood, he was a great contrast to any of the other men in Anne's life. He had loved her, too. There had never been a moment of great revelation. They had both known that they loved and that one day they would marry. Bruce had disapproved. Dennis was a younger son with few prospects, and Bruce had felt that his sunny, happy-go-lucky nature would not help him to make his way in a harsh world. But Anne would have defied Bruce and her father if he had offered any resistance when the time came. But the time never came. Dennis had ridden off to war as the greatest adventure of his life, and had died a hero's death in Spain in the Peninsular War.

Anne had no other friends. Acquaintances, yes, but no one in whom she could confide her innermost thoughts. Her natural shyness had grown on her, so that for several years she had appeared almost contented with the harsh and humorless Bruce, keeping house for him, satisfying him by avoiding any social function that he considered frivolous, and by wearing clothes so plain that she often considered that she could be mistaken for a servant. She had lost interest in almost everything that happened around her, living in a state of almost suspended animation, waiting for she knew not what. She realized occasionally, looking at herself almost without recognition in a looking glass and grimacing, that she had allowed herself to become shockingly overweight, and that it was a long, long time since she had even tried to do something with her hair, which was a rather uninteresting shade of brown anyway.

Sometimes she resolved to take herself in hand and to make the most of the few assets that she possessed. But when it came to the point, she always found herself making excuses. What was the point of spending hours creating a fashionable or attractive hairstyle when she had nowhere to display it? Anyway, Bruce would frown and accuse her of frivolity. And he liked to see her wearing caps at home. It really was not worth the effort of fighting with him. It was difficult to look attractive when one was so definitely fat. And how could she do anything about that when doing so would involve giving up food, her only indulgence?

Anne, at two-and-twenty, seemed to have given up on life. It made little difference to her whether she continued to live at the house where she had always lived, or whether she removed to the little brick school-house with Bruce. It was unlikely that he would ever marry. He had never shown any particular interest in any of the young ladies with whom they had come in contact in the previous few years, though Anne had wondered about his real feelings for her friend Sonia. She must be content, then, to spend her life looking after his needs while he provided her with the necessities of life.

The move was to be made in December, before the weather could be expected to turn harsh with winter. The belongings they were to take with them had been packed into a few trunks, the servants had been dismissed, and their own journey was to be made the day after the servants left. Both had been invited to spend their last evening with Bruce's particular friends, the Reverend Honeywell and his wife. Bruce had gone, but Anne had pleaded a whole list of last-minute tasks to be done before she could leave the following morning. To her relief, Bruce had not pressed her on the matter. She really could not have endured a whole evening of the vicar's moralizing.

The snow had taken her somewhat by surprise. Bruce had mentioned before he left that the sky was darkening and that he was likely to have to ride home through rain. But neither of them had considered snow. It seemed just a little too early in the year. But after darkness fell, when she peered through the library window to see if there was any sign of the threatened rain, she was amazed to see that the ground was completely blanketed in white already and that snow was hanging heavy from the trees that lined the driveway. During the next hour she abandoned all thought of expecting Bruce home that night. He surely would not be so foolish as to try to reach home when he had all of three miles of open country to cross. He was much more likely to stay at the vicarage and come home the next morning when he would have daylight by which to see his way.

Next she abandoned all hope of being able to travel to their new home the following day. The snow was becoming thicker by the minute and it did not look wet and ready to melt at the first ray of sunshine. This snow might stay for a while. Anne was not vastly upset by the delay. It would be inconvenient to be alone in such a large house without any servants, but she would contrive to keep herself— and Bruce when he returned—warm and fed. One consolation was that the same storm that kept them at home would also keep their new tenants from arriving. After an hour or so, Anne stopped wandering to the window and peering out. It was not a comfortable thought to be entirely alone in a large house at night, but there was an element of adventure involved. At least she would not have to worry about thieves or vagrants on such a night.

It was while she was consoling herself with this thought that the knock came on the door. It frightened Anne not a little, so loudly was the knocker banged against the door and so unexpected was the sound. She even found herself standing uncertainly in the middle of the library floor for a few moments until the loud banging sent her scurrying into the hallway. Bruce would not appreciate being kept waiting. But what could have possessed him to make the journey on a night like this? He might be somewhat worried about her being alone, but Bruce was nothing if not a prudent man. He was not in the habit of risking his own safety for the sake of gallantry.

Anne struggled with the bolts on the heavy door as her brother hammered on the other side for the third time. Finally all the bolts were drawn back and she was able to struggle with the door itself.

"Bruce," she said, "you should not have . . ." Then she saw that it was not her brother standing there but a perfect stranger, who was muffled to the eyes and whose clothes were almost completely matted with snow.

As she stood there foolishly, not knowing what to say, he brushed past her into the hallway and it was too late to think of her own safety. Not that she could have turned him away anyway. It was a wild night outside, and anyone caught out there without shelter would be in a dangerous situation indeed. If only Bruce were there, or if only she could reasonably expect him to come . . .

Her eyes quickly took in the man's fashionable and expensive clothes, his air of complete self-assurance, almost insolence, and his frightening good looks. Frightening to Anne, that was. He was tall and straight. She suspected that the many capes of that greatcoat, which was even now shedding wet snow onto the floor, hid a pair of broad and capable shoulders. His hair, she saw when he removed his beaver hat, was flattened and untidy, but the most glorious shade of near black. His face was long, his nose aquiline, his cheeks creased by laugh lines. His eyes were a decided shade of blue and did strange things to her breathing when she told him that there were no servants to stable his horse for him. He looked so directly at her.

When he went outside again to tend his horse, Anne tried desperately to gather her wits about her. She had become uncommonly shy in the past few years, especially in male company. Yet now she was very much alone with a man who could only be described as very male indeed. She was agonizingly aware suddenly of her own appearance and her total lack of charms. Why, he had looked upon her and spoken to her more as if she were a thing than a person. She supposed that the unusual circumstances and his recent escape from an extremely uncomfortable situation gave him some excuse for his imperious manner. He had almost ordered her to build up the fire and to provide him with food and drink, just as if she were a servant. But still, she thought, hurt despite her common sense, he would not have spoken to Sonia so—or even to her, had she looked more the fashionable lady.

Anne did not know what to do when the man returned to the house. His exquisite physique and perfectly tailored clothes, revealed when he removed his greatcoat, confirmed her suspicions that she was dealing with a nonpareil and destroyed any small vestige of self-assurance that remained to her. And if it had not happened then, it most certainly would have happened a moment later when he told her his name. A viscount! She had never before met a titled member of the nobility despite the fact that her grandfather had been a baron. And this man called her Anne, without so much as a by-your-leave. Perhaps the aristocracy was permitted such familiarities, she thought dubiously.

Taking his supper into the library a few minutes later was an ordeal that Anne avoided for as long as she could. Twice she picked up the tray from the kitchen table and put it down again, her heart thumping uncomfortably against her ribs. What was she to do when she got there? She would have to stay and give the viscount her company. She would have to play the hostess and converse with him. But of what would she talk? She knew nothing about London or any topic that could be of the remotest interest to him. He would see how dull and unattractive she was, and she would have the humiliation of seeing boredom and disdain on his handsome face. Finally, she picked up the tray once more and walked determinedly to the library.

Viscount Merrick had made himself comfortable in her brother's favorite chair and looked far less formidable than he had in the hallway earlier. He smiled at her with an unforced charm and invited her to be seated. It was ridiculous, of course, that he invited her to sit in her own home, but in truth she had felt awkward and had not had the presence of mind to take a seat as soon as she had set down the tray.

But Anne could think of nothing to say. She sat staring at him, aware of how foolish she must appear. She found what she had found all her life: that the more she racked her brain for an interesting topic of conversation, the blanker her mind became. She was grateful to the stranger for the way he smiled at her and seemed genuinely to appreciate the hospitality she had shown. If only he had not been quite so handsome and quite so fashionable, and if only his smile did not indicate a quite irresistible charm, perhaps she could have been more at her ease. As it was, she was so flustered that she hardly knew what she did. It was with a feeling of the utmost relief that she jumped to her feet when he suggested that she show him to his room. His experience in the storm, of course, had made him very ready to retire early. She would give him Bruce's room.

When she had put down the candlestick on the dresser, Anne was shocked to discover her guest leaning indolently in the doorway, that smile still on his face but somewhat lazier and more narrow-eyed.

The strangeness of the situation was borne in on her
with more force than before. She was alone in a
bedchamber with a strange and very masculine guest,
and they were alone in the house and likely to be for
the rest of the night. She stared at him. The impropriety of the request that she turn down his bedclothes for him at first paralyzed her, but he was an
important man from a world that was strange to her.
It was easier to comply than to take issue with the
request. Anyway, she did not feel herself at all
equipped to cross this man's will. She moved to the
bed without a murmur and folded down the blankets and sheets.

Anne felt, more than heard, that he had come up
behind her. She was frightened. Terrified, in fact.
She found it difficult to draw breath. And then his
arm came beneath her own and his fingers feathered
across her breasts. His touch was light. She hardly
felt it, but every nerve ending in her body shuddered to life. She should have whirled around and
smacked his face hard. Some remote part of her
mind even suggested that she do just that. She should
have been very frightened; there was no possible
way she could have avoided ravishment if such had
been the stranger's intention. But she was no longer
afraid. She turned to the man who had just reminded her in a flash, as she had not been reminded
in years, that she was a woman with the need to be
loved and wanted for herself.

She read curiosity and desire in his eyes before his
mouth lowered to hers. And the woman in her came
fully awake again after four years. She had not been
kissed like this since Dennis had ridden off to war.
In fact, she had not been kissed at all since that time.
And Dennis had never kissed her like this, she thought
with wonder as the viscount's mouth opened over
hers and his tongue created wonderfully erotic sen-
sations across her lips. Anne began to lose all touch
with reality. This man wanted her, and he was making
her feel desirable again. And she wanted him. She

wanted more of his kisses, more of his touch. Her body tensed with a nervous excitement as he pressed it against his own. She was going to surrender to him, she realized with a kind of lassitude over which she had no control. The thought of resistance did not really enter her consciousness at all.

But suddenly his face was above hers and he was talking to her. She stared up at him, dazed.

"Have you not been touched before, Anne?" he had said.

"My lord?"

And then he spoke words that brought her jolting back to the full and horrible reality of her situation, to the degradation of what she was doing and about to do.

"Have you had no man inside you, girl?" he said.

The words shocked her so deeply that she completely lost all control over her reactions. His words meant the same as if he had asked her if she were a virgin. But they so graphically described what she had been about to do—with a complete stranger.

She hardly heard the gentle words of reassurance, hardly comprehended that she was not going to be taken by force. The only fact that she did realize finally was that he had stood aside and was indicating that he expected her to leave. Anne fled. And it was many hours before she fell into a fitful sleep. Her mind wrestled with her emotions. She had behaved with shocking impropriety, her mind said. She had almost given herself to a man she had met only a few hours before, without even a struggle. Indeed, she would have done so had he not held back. She had been found desirable, her emotions said, and by a man who could surely have his pick of any of the most eligible ladies of the *ton*. She had been held and kissed and caressed until she had felt alive and feminine again. She almost wished that he had not stopped.

She did not know what the morning would bring. In all likelihood Viscount Merrick would leave as soon as the snow had melted enough to make the roads passable. She would never see him again. But surely he had given her the incentive she needed to come out of the sleep that had lasted far too long. She was a woman and still young. She could never be a beauty, but she could make herself at least passable if she lost weight and if she made an effort to dress and to style her hair more fashionably. Anne fell asleep, somewhat comforted by her resolve.

3 "I-I don't understand, my lord," Anne Parrish said. Her hands were unconsciously twisting the sides of her gray wool dress as she stared at the viscount's straight back.

Viscount Merrick was in the library, standing at the window. His back was to the room. He stared out at the snow that still blanketed the gardens outside, even though water was already dripping from the roof. He did not immediately answer her unstated query. Finally, he turned to face her, a smile on his rather white face.

"I meant just what I said, Miss Parrish," he said. "Have you never had an offer of marriage before? I would be honored if you will consent to become my wife. Is that clear enough for you? And will you, ma'am ?"

Anne continued to stare. The words, though repeated, still refused to register themselves fully on her mind. Marriage! He was asking her to marry him. She had dreamed of such an ending the night before during several waking spells. How wonderful it would be, she had thought, to be swept off her feet by this very romantic and very handsome stranger, who was a viscount, no less. How marvelous it would be if he fell in love with her and took her away with him to the large home and estate she was sure he must own, and to London, where she would find herself in the middle of the life of the *haut ton*. She would lose weight and he would buy her fashionable clothes. Suddenly, under the influence of his love, she would no longer be shy, no longer tongue-tied in the company of strangers. She would be vivacious and dazzling. His friends and acquaintances would envy him and want to know where he had found such a treasure.

Anne had actually chuckled aloud at herself when the dreams reached the point at which she was chatting amiably to an admiring Prince Regent, who insisted that she sit at his right hand during a dinner in Carlton House because he found all his other guests such bores. It was all very well to be a dreamer; visions of romance could help make a very dull life more bearable. But it was another matter to attach those dreams to a very live man who happened to be sleeping in a room in one's own house and whom one had to meet again in the morning.

But this was not a dream. She was fully awake in the library, the most familiar room in the house. The logs were crackling in the fireplace. And the breathless nervousness she was feeling was not the sort of reaction that she ever felt in her dreams. In those, she was always very much in command of a situation. Viscount Merrick had asked her to marry him. She took a deep breath.

"I do not understand," she said again. "You do not know me, my lord."

He moved from the window and came to stand a few feet in front of her, his hands clasped behind his back. Anne was very much aware of his intensely blue eyes looking into hers. "Not very well, it is true," he agreed, "but I have seen enough to appreciate your hospitality and your kind heart. I believe we will deal well together. And I have your brother's permission to pay my addresses to you."

"Bruce?" she said, dazed. "You have asked Bruce?"

"Yes, indeed," he said, and smiled anew. "Did you believe I was asking you to run away to Gretna Green with me?"

"Oh, there would be no need," she said seriously, a split second before she realized that she was being teased. "I am of age, you know."

"Well, then," he said, "what is your answer to be? Will you marry me, Anne?"

She looked back at him earnestly, trying to discern from the expression on his face the reason behind this strange turn of events. She had been in the kitchen earlier that morning when the viscount had come downstairs, looking quite immaculate despite the fact that he wore the same clothes as the night before. He was even shaved. Anne guessed that his shaving gear was in the leather bag that he had carried with him when he arrived. She had been trying to cook eggs and ham over the stove, which had taken her a long time to light earlier. Fortunately, he had made no adverse comment on the lack of variety that their breakfast was to offer. He had merely told her to bring the food to the dining room as soon as it was ready, and had wandered off again.

He had invited her to join him at the table when she took the food in on a tray, looking as amused as he had the night before when she had hesitated about joining him. But he had made little attempt to converse with her, beyond a compliment on the quality of the coffee she had brewed. He had browsed through an old periodical that he must have brought from the library.

Bruce had arrived home as she was carrying the dishes from the room. He had walked all the way from the village, wading up to his knees in places, he said. But he had felt compelled to make the attempt, knowing that his sister was alone at home. The vicar had come with him, refusing to allow his friend out into the white world without some companionship. Anne had taken them into the dining room, where the viscount was still hidden behind his periodical, and had introduced the three men. She had left the room with the loaded tray just after the guest had leapt to his feet and flung his periodical to the table. That was the last she had seen of him until Bruce had come to her in the kitchen and told her to go to the library.

Anne had quickly dried her hands and gone. Bruce was clearly in one of his moods. He was grim and tight-lipped. Clearly he considered her behavior bad-mannered in the extreme. It must be that he expected her to remain with their guests, smiling and trying desperately to think of something to say. He could not understand that in the absence of servants work piled up. Someone had to keep the house tidy, cook the meals, and wash the dishes.

But when she reached the library, it was to find only the viscount there. And suddenly she was "Miss Parrish." And he had made her a formal proposal of marriage. It was all most romantic and utterly frightening—and downright impossible.

"Yes," she stammered. "I mean, if you really wish it and if Bruce has given his consent. Yes, I would be honored. If you truly wish it, that is. My lord." Like a schoolgirl. Gone was the Anne of the daydreams.

The smile and the charm were gone from his face instantly. He almost snapped to attention. His jaw clenched. "Then that is settled," he said matter-of-factly. "How fortunate it is that your brother chose to bring a clergyman with him this morning, since it seems that we will be housebound for at least the rest of today. We will be able to make arrangements with him to be wed within the next few days, and I shall be able to take you to Redlands as soon as the roads are passable again."

"Within the next few days?" Anne echoed faintly. "You wish to be married so soon, my lord? Do you not have family members that you wish to have present?"

"Not at all," he said briskly. "I have always considered elaborate weddings to be an utter foolishness. A church and a minister and a couple of witnesses are quite sufficient to make a binding marriage. It will be time enough for my family to be informed when the deed is accomplished."

This was not the stuff of dreams at all. There was to be no large church, then, and no crowds of admiring guests and laughing well-wishers afterward. Just the village church and the Reverend Honeywell and Bruce. But did it really matter? Was there not something unutterably romantic about the notion of taking the fashionable world by storm? She would be introduced to his family and his friends as his wife. How surprised they would all be! If only she had a chance first to lose some weight and to improve her wardrobe. But no matter. She would do both in the course of the next few months, and even the viscount would be surprised to discover that his wife could be attractive.

The viscount! She did not know his given name. She blushed with embarrassment as she looked up at him. Would he think of telling her? It was impossible to ask him when she was already betrothed to him.

He observed her blush unsmilingly. "Since you have been stranded here without servants, ma'am," he said, "I can imagine that you must have a thousand and one tasks to occupy your time. I must not keep you. I shall discuss the arrangements for our nuptials with your brother and the vicar, and refer them to you later for your approval." He took Anne's hand, which was still pleating the stuff of her gown, straightened her fingers with his own strong hand, and raised them briefly to his lips.

Left alone in the library, Viscount Merrick crossed again to the window and stared unseeingly out at the snow, his hands clasped behind his back. His mind and his feelings were as frozen as the world without. Even more so. There was water dripping from the

eaves across his line of vision. There was no comfort
at all for him.

How, in heaven's name, had he got himself into
such a coil? He still could not quite convince himself
that he was not asleep, locked into some nightmare
from which he could not shake himself loose. Yesterday—just a matter of hours ago, in fact—he had
been riding with as much haste as he could muster to
London and Lorraine. Their betrothal was to be
announced within the week. He was to be back in the
world he knew and loved, the world with which he
felt thoroughly comfortable. He had been annoyed
to think that the storm might delay his return to that
world by so much as a day. He had considered the
appearance of this house a stroke of good fortune
once he had accepted the necessity of that delay.

But now! He was betrothed to a girl whom he
found in no way attractive, honor-bound to marry
her within the next few days, sentenced to spend the
rest of his life shackled to her. A girl whom he had
considered to be a servant until a very few hours
ago.

The events of the last couple of hours were so
jumbled in his mind that he had hardly sorted out
yet what had happened. He did remember that when
the brother had arrived in the dining room and been
introduced, he had not needed to inquire if he was
the owner or a servant left in charge. The answer
was very obvious. And he had realized in a flash that
Anne was no servant, either. Her speech was quite
genteel. He should have noticed that instead of drawing his conclusions entirely from her mode of dress.
He should have known from experience that in the
country people did not always dress according to
their station. It did not take Merrick long to learn—
from the Reverend Honeywell—that brother and sister were the grandchildren of a baron and close
relatives of the present holder of the title.

Merrick's first thought had been one of relief. He
had come uncomfortably close to compromising a

lady's honor. It was no servant girl that he had almost seduced the night before. But the feeling was short-lived. It soon became very obvious that both Parrish and the vicar considered that the girl's honor had indeed been compromised very badly. She had spent a night alone with him, and even though they did not suspect him of having behaved in an ungentlemanly fashion, and even though they knew that Anne's behavior was always above reproach ... Merrick had not listened to every word or argument. But their meaning had been patently clear. The only way the situation could be redeemed was for the two who had been alone together to be wed.

He could have resisted, Merrick supposed now, watching a heavy pile of snow finally lose its hold on the bare branch of an oak tree and crash to the ground. It was quite ridiculous really to suppose that honor was compromised when circumstances as drastic as those of the night before had forced two people into company together. It was not even as if they had been trapped together in a single room. They had been in a large house that must have at least eight bedchambers. Why would the proper minds of those who would hear of the incident suppose that they had occupied only one of those rooms? Such a notion of honor was old-fashioned, and rightly so.

Yet somehow it is not so easy to resist when one is faced by the righteous and tight-lipped owner of a house with which one has made free for a night and a morning. Especially when that owner is accompanied by a very sober and stern-looking country vicar who stares at one as if he can see a devil and its pitchfork over one's shoulder. And more especially when one knows oneself not entirely blameless. It still seemed miraculous to Merrick that he had not bedded the girl when he had so obviously overcome any resistance that she might have offered.

Almost in a dream, he had agreed that the honorable thing to do was to offer for the girl. Before the idea had had a chance to take root in his mind, before he had had time to realize that he would lose Lorraine and all his dreams for the future, Merrick found himself in the library awaiting the arrival of the girl. Even then he had not realized the finality of the situation. Surely she would laugh at the notion of marrying a complete stranger and moving away with him. She would refuse him. Gallantry dictated that he treat her with courtesy. He had found when confronted with her that he could not be wholly truthful and explain that he was offering only because her brother and the vicar considered it the honorable course for him to take. He had had to pretend that he really wished the match.

But surely she should have realized the truth. She must know that in real life men did not that easily make a decision to marry a strange girl. She must know that she was a dowd whom no man in his right mind could fall for within the course of a few hours. He expected her to reject him, had not dared to think of what he would be facing if she accepted. His mind had become completely numbed by her reply. He could hardly recall now what he had said or how he had behaved toward her. Had his natural courtesy of manner prevented him from showing the horror and disgust that he had been feeling?

Merrick watched the snow outside the window become wetter. Soon it would melt off the roadways. There was the faintest chance that by late afternoon it would be possible to travel again. But the thought brought no comfort. He would be going nowhere for the next few days, not until after his wedding, and then he would have to make arrangements for his wife to travel with him. His wife! That little drab of a girl who even now looked to him all the world like a servant. What was he to do with her? He could not possibly take her back with him to London. The very thought of being seen with her by all his acquaintances, of having to face Lorraine with her, made him feel nauseated.

And as he stood there by the window, a faint

suspicion began to form in Merrick's mind and to grow by the minute. He had fallen surely into a cleverly laid trap. Miss Anne Parrish might be completely lacking in feminine attractions, but she had considerable intelligence. She must have seen almost immediately the night before how she could turn the situation to her advantage. She must have seen that he had mistaken her for a servant, yet she had made no attempt to correct his error. She had played along with his mistake, acting the part with great skill. She must have realized, little dowd that she was, that this was the great chance of her life. If she could only seduce him—yes, indeed, it was she who had been the seducer—she would be able to force him into marriage.

She had succeeded, of course, much better than she could have expected. She had kept her honor intact and yet still won her point. Perhaps she had realized that, too. She must know her brother and that vicar fellow pretty well. She would have realized that in their narrow-minded view of life even the fact that he had spent the night in the same house as she would mean that her honor had been compromised. It had really been easy for her. All she had had to do was ensure that he stayed at the house all night and long enough the next day for her brother to come home and find him there.

The more he thought of the matter, the more Merrick was convinced that he had discovered the truth. Why else would the girl have accepted him with such little reluctance? Of course, he had introduced himself the night before by his title, obviously a great mistake. He was wearing his most fashionable and expensive clothes. He must have appeared a great catch indeed. And what a foolish one! He might have known that country morality was far more straitlaced than that to which he was more accustomed. He should have pressed on the night before after warming himself in the house. She had told him that the village was a mere three miles

away. It surely would not have been impossible to
travel that far. But, of course, he could not have
been expected to foresee the danger; he had taken
her for a servant. And he could not really blame
himself for that. She certainly looked every inch the
part, and she was a skilled actress. Only her speech
might have given her away.

Merrick found that he was clenching and unclench-
ing his hands at his sides and that his teeth were so
firmly clamped together that his jaw ached. It was all
true. Reality was beginning to establish its hold on
his mind. He was not dreaming. Within the course
of a few hours, his whole life had changed. All his
dreams and plans for the future were ruined, and
his new plans hardly bore contemplation. He had
committed himself to this girl and would have to
marry her. But he was damned if he would pretend
to like it. His life might never be able to take the
course that he had planned, but he was not going to
allow the scheming little chit to ruin it altogether.
She would be made to feel very sorry indeed for
what she had done. She might bear his name and his
title, but she would gain nothing else from this marriage if he had anything to say in the matter.

Anne Parrish and Alexander Stewart, Viscount
Merrick, were married two days later in the village
church. The Reverend Honeywell officiated, and Mrs.
Honeywell and Bruce Parrish witnessed the ceremony. No one else was present or even knew of the
wedding. The new tenants of the house had not yet
arrived, and the present occupants had been nowhere during the days that intervened between the
morning after the storm and that of the nuptials.
The vicar's wife served tea and cakes in the vicarage
afterward, but the viscount refused the offer of a
wedding meal. He had hired a carriage with which
to take his bride to his home in Wiltshire and intended to start without further delay. Even so, the

state of the roads made it uncertain that they would complete the journey before nightfall.

Anne had never thought that she would feel sorry to say good-bye to her brother and to the home where she had never known much of happiness. But she felt something very near to panic as the shabby coach, the best the village had for hire, drew away from the gate of the vicarage and the group of three standing there waving to her. Only then was it fully borne in on her that the man beside her—her husband—was a stranger. And a very quiet stranger at that. In the last couple of days, though they had occupied the same house, they had spent almost no time in each other's company and no time at all alone. She had been busy in the kitchen much of the time. He had spent a great deal of time outside, either in the stable endlessly grooming his horse or in the grounds of the house trudging through the snow. He had spent very little time even with Bruce, seeming to prefer to be alone.

And that morning he had sat beside her in the coach, the same one in which they traveled now, Bruce on the seat facing them, saying not a word, making no attempt to touch her, or to smile at her, or to offer any sign at all that she was his bride and that they were on their way to be married.

Her bewilderment had grown during those two days to the point at which she did not know what to think. All the charm that he had used in the library when he had asked her to marry him had disappeared without trace. Since that time he had shown no interest in her, had acted indeed as if he were unaware of her existence. Yet he had made no move to explain to her that he had not been serious about his offer or that he regretted it and wanted to withdraw from his commitment. Why had he offered? He must have wanted her when he spoke to her. Was he perhaps merely feeling awkward at being trapped for a few days in a house without a change of clothes and without any of the people he knew?

Yet it had been his decision that they marry there in such haste.

Perhaps now that they were on their way to Redlands—his home, about which she knew nothing except the name—he would be different. She waited for him to speak, to turn to her with some warmth. She expected him to begin to tell her about his home and family, about himself. Yet he sat straight on his seat, not touching her, looking out onto the dull world of melting snow and mud. And Anne dared not speak herself. She could think of nothing to say that would be sure to break down his reserve. So she stared out of her window, tense, uncomfortable, feeling the silence grow between them like a tangible thing.

4 Viscount Merrick and his bride arrived at Redlands at dusk. They were quite unexpected. The butler, Dodd, and the housekeeper, Mrs. Rush, always ran a strict establishment. No holland covers over the furniture in the best rooms for them. The servants were kept as busy when the master was from home as they were when he was in residence. The house was kept as immaculately clean. But it was a shabby house. The viscount had never made it a principal residence and had never taken any great interest in its decoration or upkeep. The gardens, similarly, were kept neat around the house by a hardworking gardener, but no one had ever taken the initiative to make anything beautiful of the extensive grounds.

When a dilapidated carriage was seen, then, by a groom, to be driving toward the house, and when the master himself was seen to alight and to turn to help a lady to descend, there was considerable excitement and curiosity, but no panic. Dodd pulled at his waistcoat to make sure that it was free of creases, and smoothed back the little hair that remained to him. Mrs. Rush shook out her white apron and inspected it quickly for spots. She ran her hands around the lacy brim of her cap to make sure that it was

straight on her head. Both were standing in the
hallway, flanked by the marble busts that had been
painstakingly collected by the former viscount, when
a footman finally opened the door to the travelers.
Dodd bowed stiffly from the waist; Mrs. Rush curtsied, her lined face wreathed in a smile of greeting.

"Welcome home, my lord," Dodd said in his most
stately fashion.

"Such weather, my lord," Mrs. Rush added. "We
must be thankful to the good Lord for bringing you
safely here."

Both glanced curiously at Anne.

"May I present my wife, the viscountess?" Merrick
said, and watched with unsmiling eyes the quickly
concealed amazement of the two elderly and faithful
servants. He must become accustomed to such reactions, especially from those who would see her. Fortunately for himself, he did not intend that many
people would do so—for the present, at least.

Mrs. Rush jumped into action. "You will be cold
and tired, my lady," she said. "Come to the drawing
room. There is always a fire in there from early
afternoon. I shall have a tray of tea brought up to
you at once. You must be longing for one. I shall
have your bedchamber made up immediately and
some nice hot bricks put between the sheets." She
was already bustling up the wide curved staircase
ahead of her new mistress, while Merrick lingered in
the hall to give some instructions to Dodd and to see
that his wife's boxes were removed from the carriage
and carried upstairs.

Anne was feeling tired and bewildered. The journey had been a tedious one. They had made only
one brief stop for a change of horses. Although she
had had tea, she had not been invited to alight from
the carriage. The refreshments had been brought
out to the carriage for her. The atmosphere had not
improved as the day advanced. Her husband had
remained silent. She did not believe that they had
exchanged ten sentences during the whole journey.

It was puzzling and hurtful. She knew that she should have said something, asked him what was the matter. She should have done so before the wedding ceremony, in fact. There was certainly something very strange about his attitude. But she had not done so. She was far too timid. It was very easy in her mind to be positive, to take the initiative. In real life she allowed herself to be swept along by the plans of other people.

Now she found herself in the very uncomfortable position of being in a strange house, of which she supposed she was now mistress, with a strange man who was her husband but whom she knew not at all. And she had the growing suspicion that he did not really welcome her presence. However, as she followed the housekeeper up the stairs and along the hallway to a warm and large drawing room, she felt a measure of comfort. Mrs. Rush was friendly and seemed genuinely concerned for her comfort. She chattered constantly as she walked. Anne smiled with gratitude as she allowed her gray cloak and bonnet to be removed and a chair to be drawn closer to the dancing flames of the fire. It seemed to be years since anyone had fussed over her. Their servants at home had been chosen by Bruce and generally had his own sternness of manner.

"Thank you, Mrs. Rush," she said. "I have never been so glad in my life to see a fire. All I need to complete my happiness is a cup of tea."

The housekeeper smiled back. "I shall have a whole pot sent up right away, my lady," she said, "and a plate of currant cakes that Cook made fresh this afternoon. It was almost as if she knew you were coming."

She bustled from the room and soon had the cook and two chambermaids rushing around to produce the promised refreshments without delay. All the while, she gave it as her opinion that the master had chosen himself a very good sort of a girl for a bride. Not one of your grand ladies that was all frills and curls and never a sensible or a kindly thought in her

mind. "Though I was never more surprised in my
life," she added. "I always expected that his lordship
would marry a beauty. In fact, it has been rumored
that he was about to get himself betrothed to a marquess's daughter. I can't think why he has suddenly
gone and got himself wed to someone we have never
heard of. She has only two trunks, too, and no maid.
But a very sweet lady, if my judgment is correct."

No one suggested that perhaps it was not. Mrs.
Rush's word and her opinion were law belowstairs at
Redlands. Only Dodd would ever have dared to dis-
pute any of her pronouncements, and fortunately
for the peace of the house, these two leaders of the
household almost invariably agreed on all major topics. Thus it was that Anne Stewart, Viscountess of
Merrick, was favorably received by the servants of
her new home, at least.

She was unaware of this, however, having felt only
the early kindliness of Mrs. Rush. She drank her tea
and ate her cakes alone in the drawing room, gazing
around her almost timidly, as if she were spying into
a place where she had no business to be. Her mind
registered the largeness and airiness of the room,
which was somewhat spoiled by the shabbiness of
wall tapestries that had been bleached by the sun-
light of most of their color, of carpets that were
worn in the places where they were most trodden
and therefore most exposed to view, and of furniture that was heavy and inelegant. Strangely, it was a
cosy room, but she felt strongly that it must be a long
time since anyone had taken any real pride in the
appearance of the house. The fact surprised her.
Even in the gathering dusk, she had been able to see
as they had approached the house that it was far
more magnificent and the grounds far more extensive than even she had pictured them in her imagination.

She did not know what to do when her second cup
of tea was finished and still she was alone. She began
to have painful visions of being forgotten there and

of finally having to make up her mind to leave the room and find out where she was to go next. It was with great relief that she turned to the opening door and saw Mrs. Rush bustle in again.

"If you are warm and ready to leave the fire, my lady," she said, "I shall show you to your chamber. You need not fear that it will be unaired. I always see to it that there is a fire in the room twice a week and that bricks are put into the bed just as often. You will find a cheerful fire there now, and Bella has unpacked your boxes already and had everything put away for you. She will be your maid until you wish to make other arrangements. His lordship says that will be suitable, and I am sure that you will, like Bella. She dresses a head better than any ladies' maid I know, and she is a very cheerful sort of a girl. She does not talk your head off when you are trying to think of other things, like some servants I could name."

Anne smiled and allowed herself to be led away and to be fussed. It was from the housekeeper that she learned that dinner would be served at eight, and that presumably she would see her husband again that night. She had begun to wonder. Certainly it was proving to be a far stranger wedding day than she had ever imagined. Even during the past two days, when the viscount had been so silent, she had imagined that everything would be well once they were married and alone. She had conceded that he was in a very awkward position, living in a house that was not his own, constantly in the presence of her brother whenever he came indoors. He would be smiling and charming once more after their wedding, she had thought, and would show once again that he appreciated her as a woman. But she still waited.

The meal proved to be as painful as the journey eaarlier in the day had been. They sat in a very formal dining room at a table that would have seated

twenty quite comfortably. Merrick sat at one end,
Anne at the other. Even if they had wished to converse, they would have had to raise their voices to an
unnatural pitch. But they exchanged hardly a word.
Anne was constantly aware of the butler and a single
footman almost ceaselessly walking between them
bearing bowls and tureens, removing dishes of food
that had hardly been touched. She looked anxiously
down the table when the last course had been carried away. Did he expect her now to leave him alone
with his port? Fortunately, Merrick picked up his
cue on this occasion.

"I have given instructions that the fire in the drawing room need not be built up," he said. "I assume
you are tired after our long journey?"

"Yes, my lord," she agreed. "I shall be glad to
retire early to bed." And she blushed as she said the
words. Was this part of the wedding day, at least, to
be normal? Was there to be a wedding night? She
noticed with sudden clarity his extreme handsome-
ness. He was no longer in the expensive but severe
riding clothes that he had worn for the last several
days, including his wedding, but in a russet satin coat
over a gold brocade waistcoat and crisp white shirt
with an elaborately tied neckcloth. His near-black
hair was freshly washed and was brushed back in
thick, soft waves from his face. The severity of his
expression merely served to emphasize his quite dev-
astating good looks.

She was equally aware of her own appearance. She
wore a silk dress of olive green, her best, but she
knew that its high neckline and natural waistline
were not fashionable. And the plainness of the design served only to emphasize her unflattering plump-
ness. She was aware of her hair, which Bella had
tried valiantly to coax into feminine ringlets, but
which looked far too young with her round face. She
felt hopelessly inferior.

"I shall follow you up in a short while," Merrick
said stiffly, answering one of Anne's questions, at

least. She left the room, hoping that her blush was not as obvious to the eye as it felt.

Merrick lifted to his lips the glass of port that Dodd had just filled for him, and stared ahead. It was far worse than he had expected. He could not understand now why he had allowed it all to happen. He should have made a firm stand right from the start. Bruce Parrish and the Reverend Honeywell should have been made to understand that Anne had extended only a very necessary hospitality to him on the night of the storm, that his very survival had depended on his staying there at the house. It had been quite ridiculous to claim that honor demanded that they marry. He should have pointed out to them in no uncertain terms that he was already betrothed, that he could not change the course of his whole life just to suit their strange notions of propriety. Miss Parrish's reputation need not be tarnished, anyway, if they chose to say nothing of the matter. No one knew of it except the four of them.

Instead, he had allowed himself to be manipulated by them just as if he had no will of his own. He found it difficult to understand himself. He was usually a leader, not a follower. He had never thought of himself as having a weak will. The worst of it was that he was more than ever convinced that he had been used very cleverly by Anne herself. His wife! She was so quiet, so timid. He had found annoyance growing against her all day. It was all so artificial. She was a clever little schemer, he was convinced, a woman quite capable of getting what she wanted without having any good looks or character with which to do so. He had waited all day for her to show her true self. Sitting beside her in the carriage, he had waited for her to begin to talk, to show her satisfaction in what she had achieved. He had waited for her triumphant reaction to the house, which was one of the most imposing in the country, though he had to admit that it was somewhat shabby.

The fact that she still persisted in the timid, innocent behavior that she had shown from the beginning only served to make him more irritated. This woman was his wife, yet she had never shown anything of her true self to him. This was his wedding night. Merrick gritted his teeth and motioned to Dodd to refill his glass. He hastily tried to drown out images of Lorraine as he had imagined her on such an occasion. He had not sent word to her or to anyone of the change in his state. He did not know how he was going to do so.

But he did know that he could not stay here. Redlands had never been a home to him. It had been his since the death of his father, but because he had been an infant at the time, he had been taken to live with his grandparents, visiting his own home only on rare occasions. By the time he grew up, the place had grown to look sadly neglected, and his own youthful tastes had run to more social pleasures than the country estate could supply. Under ordinary circumstances he would not have dreamed of bringing his bride here. It was not his idea of an ideal site for a honeymoon. He would not be able to face living here for any length of time.

At the same time, he could not face taking his wife to London. The Season would not begin for a few months yet, but the capital was crowded enough already now that winter had come. He would have to take her to numerous social activities, introduce her to the *ton*. His friends would see her. She would meet Lorraine and her parents. No, it was quite impossible. How could he bear to see the surprise and derision in everyone's eyes when they learned that he had wed in such haste a girl whom he would not normally afford a second glance? How could he bear to see her next to Lorraine and be painfully reminded of what he had lost? The contrast between them would be almost laughable: Lorraine tall and slim, exquisitely dressed, beautiful, while Anne was small and plump, dowdily clothed, and quite plain.

Merrick decided as he sat there that he would

return to London alone the next day. The decision
had really been made a few days before, but now he
made the conscious choice. His wife would stay at
Redlands. Who would blame him? It was quite common for wives to be left in the country while husbands lived in London. The house was quite comfortable and well-run. He would make her a generous allowance. She had achieved what she wanted.
She had his name and his title, and was assured of a
comfortably secure future. That had been her goal,
Merrick was convinced. He had learned in the few
days he had spent at her brother's home that they
were impoverished. If only he had traveled one day
later, they would not even have been in the area but
at a village thirty miles distant, where his wife's brother
had taken up a position as a schoolmaster. If only he
had listened to Horace!

Merrick twirled his empty glass in his hand and
resisted the idea of motioning to Dodd again. This
was his wedding night and tomorrow he would be
gone. The marriage must be consummated. He could
not have the girl writing to her brother or to that
vicar complaining that she had been cheated, that
hers was no proper marriage. Distasteful as the idea
was, he must go to her. And, since go he must, there
was nothing to be gained from delay. He put the
glass down on the table and pushed himself to his
feet.

Anne was standing beside the high bed when
Merrick entered the room from the dressing room
that joined their two rooms. She was looping back
the heavy blue curtains that surrounded the bed,
looking timid and hesitant, as if she did not know
whether she should climb into the bed or not. He
stood in the doorway for a moment, his hand on the
knob, taking in with some distaste her most unbride-
like appearance. She wore a long and loose nightgown of white flannel, quite unadorned. It hung
shapeless around her plump figure. She wore no

nightcap; her hair had been brushed loose about her shoulders. It framed a round and anxious face that appeared far too childish for her years. She was two-and-twenty, her brother had informed him. Merrick closed the door quietly behind him.

"I expected to find you abed already," he said as he approached her.

"No," she said. "I have been trying to pull back these curtains. I suffer from fear of suffocation when I am enclosed in too small a space, my lord."

"Then you must instruct Mrs. Rush to remove them altogether tomorrow," Merrick said, and put back with one hand the hair that hung over one of her shoulders. His knuckles brushed the nape of her neck.

"I would not wish to appear too demanding so soon," Anne said breathlessly, hardly aware of what she said. His lips were against the hollow between her shoulder and neck, his breath warm against her skin.

"Nonsense," he said. "You are mistress here now, as I am sure you fully realize. You must begin your relations with the servants as you mean to go on."

His hands moved to her breasts as he looked down into her upturned and dazed face. They were as firm and as feminine as they had felt during the light, exploratory touch he had permitted himself just a few nights previously. Merrick half-smiled down at his bride. He wanted to humiliate, even hurt her. She had schemed to acquire him as a husband. Let her take the consequences, find that she had a husband who would not be content with a discreet exercise of his rights. He lowered his head to hers, took her mouth beneath his parted lips, and nibbled lightly at her lips until they relaxed.

This time he found that his probing tongue met no resistance. He ravished her mouth, one hand spread firmly behind her head. His other hand still fondled one breast, teasing the nipple erect, reaching to undo the buttons that held her nightgown primly closed to the neck. He was hardly aware of the fact that her passivity was gradually melting, that her head angled against his own and her mouth opened wide to his invasion, that her shoulder shrugged aside the nightgown to assist his pushing hand, that her body, naked from the waist up, molded itself eagerly against the brocade of his dressing gown. He was too much involved in the desire that had swept over him in a flood and that made him forget for the time all else except that he held a woman whom he wanted with a passion that was not to be denied. He turned her in his arms and tumbled her to the bed.

Anne reached out for him in bewilderment, feeling bereft. But he had not left her. He was merely shrugging out of his dressing gown and pulling off his nightshirt. She gazed at him through passion-heavy eyes, quite unembarrassed, aware only of male beauty and of the blood that was hammering through her veins and against her temples. She did not for a moment think of covering her nakedness, but instead lifted her hips when he reached down to remove the nightgown that still clung around her. He did not extinguish the candles before coming down on top of her on the bed.

Dreams could never begin to capture the wonder of it all: his long-fingered hands exploring and caressing, finding out unerringly the places that made her ache with longing; his mouth and tongue, which claimed her own and that left hot trails of desire along her throat and on her breasts; his body, so warm and firm and heavy on her own; and his legs, which pushed firmly between her own. And then the moment of entry, so often imagined with terror, so wonderful beyond imagining. She was quite unaware of pain, all her desire culminating in the blazing shock of invasion.

She felt no reluctance. Anne knew in that moment that she loved her husband with all her being, with all the feelings that had been frozen inside her since the death of Dennis. She opened herself to him, lifted her legs from the bed so that he might thrust more deeply into her, and wrapped her arms around the firm muscles of his shoulders and back. She shuddered against him and stifled her cry of fulfillment against his shoulder moments before his full weight pressed her into the bed as he pushed himself deep inside her and gradually relaxed.

Anne was the first to recover conscious thought. Her husband was still lying heavily on top of her. His weight made it difficult for her to breathe freely. But she lay very still, staring up at the shadows cast on the canopy of the bed by the candles. She did not want to move, did not want him to stir. It was a more wonderful wedding night than any she could have dreamed for herself. All was well. The unease she had felt for the last few days and during this day had been unnecessary. He had just proved to her that he desired her, that he wanted her as a wife. She could not feel more beautiful if she had all the most lovely clothes in the world and the most sylphlike figure. He had made her beautiful with his hands and his lips and his body. He had worshiped her. She was filled with wonder. She did not know why it was so. She was not beautiful and he was. It was impossible to imagine a man who could be more so. But somehow it had happened. He had seen beyond the outer appearance to the Anne beneath, and he loved her.

She moved her head slightly until she could feel his thick hair against her cheek. She closed her eyes and concentrated on holding back the tears that wanted to flow. She must not let him see her cry. He might misinterpret her tears. She reveled in the discomfort of his weight on her.

Merrick awoke with a slight start. He had never fallen asleep on a woman before. Most females he knew would have pushed him away long ago. He lifted himself away from his wife with something like reluctance and lay beside her. He turned his head to look at her and found that she was looking back with steady gray eyes. She was the same unattractive Anne; she looked even more childish, in fact, with her cheeks flushed and her hair in tangled disarray. Was it possible that he had felt such desire for her only a few minutes before? It must have been sheer lust, he decided. She had not a single one of the attractions he always demanded in his women.

She smiled and touched his arm lightly. Merrick did not return either gesture, but he did feel an unease. Where had been the punishment? She had enjoyed the consummation; he could recall that clearly. In fact, it was partly her response that had enflamed his own desires. She had not been shocked by his unnecessary intimacies or embarrassed at being stripped of her clothes while the candles burned. Yet she had been undoubtedly virgin. He had still to show her that she had made an unwise move in trapping Alexander Stewart into matrimony.

The problem was too tricky a one to consider at the moment. He would decide what to do when he returned to his own room. Later. He leaned across to the table on which the candlestick was set and blew out the lights, then curled back into the warmth of the bed for a few minutes. He slept.

Anne was alone when she awoke the following morning, but the dented pillow and the ruffled bed-clothes beside her showed clearly that her husband had slept there. Her husband! How easily the thought had come to her mind, and how impossible it had seemed even a week ago that she would ever marry. She stretched lazily in the bed, enjoying the warmth that lingered beneath the bedclothes even though her nose told her that the room was cold. No one had yet been to build the fire in her room. She did not care. She felt wonderful: alive, beautiful, and loved. Nothing could ever be the same again. She now had a reason for making herself physically attractive. But she was almost glad that she was at present looking her worst. The fact proved to her that her husband loved her for herself. How delightful it would be to watch his pleasure when he saw her as she would be in a few months' time—or even a few weeks, if she set her mind to it.

Bella entered the room at that moment carrying a cup of steaming chocolate on a tray. "Good morning, my lady," she said, smiling knowingly at her mistress and at the tumbled bed around her. She busied herself at the fireplace, clearing the ashes from last night's fire.

"Is his lordship at breakfast yet?" Anne asked eagerly.

"He finished a while ago, my lady," the maid replied, "and sent word that he wishes to speak with you in the morning room as soon as it is convenient."

Anne smiled radiantly and flung back the bedclothes despite the chill of the room. "I must dress immediately, then," she said. "Will you help me, Bella? I do not know where you have hidden all my clothes."

A mere ten minutes later she was tripping down the stairs, a new spring in her step. She even forgot to feel embarrassed when she reached the hallway and realized that she did not know where the morning room was. She had to ask a footman.

She entered the room in a rush, smiling with bright amusement. She was all ready to share the joke of not knowing her way around her own home. She must ask her husband to show it to her if he was not too busy. If he was, then she would have Mrs. Rush perform the task. She had liked the housekeeper the night before.

Merrick was standing with his back to the fire, his hands clasped behind him. He was not smiling. "Good morning, ma'am," he said. "I trust you slept well?"

She smiled a little uncertainly. "Yes, indeed," she said. "I did not even hear you get up." She blushed.

Merrick regarded her without any change of expression. "I rose early," he said. "I had a great deal to do before I could leave today."

"Leave?"

"I shall be leaving for London within the hour," he said. "Alone."

There was a moment of silence. "When may I expect your return?" Anne asked, her smile gone.

"You may not," Merrick said. "I have no plans to return in the near future."

"Am I to join you later?" she asked hesitantly.

"No," he said. "You are to remain here."

They stared at each other. "I don't understand," Anne said at last. "I am your wife."

"Precisely," Merrick said. "I would say you have gained what you set out to achieve, ma'am. Now you may enjoy your triumph at your leisure."

Anne swallowed painfully. "What do you mean, my lord?"

"You knew as soon as you saw me, did you not," he said, "that you could use the occasion in order to trap for yourself an eligible husband? Even if your plan to lure me into bed failed, you knew that your brother would force me into feeling honor-bound to offer for you. It must have seemed a stroke of unexpected luck that he also brought with him that dry stick of a vicar to echo his moral indictment of my behavior in staying all night in a house alone with you. Well, my dear, you succeeded. I am your husband. But by God, ma'am, I shall not be subjected to having to look at you and converse with you every day of my life. I wish you joy of your new home."

Anne appeared frozen to the spot. She heard what he said, knew the truth of what had happened, realized the nightmare future that faced her, but could not force her body to adjust to the new facts. She would collapse if she could not hold the awful truth at arms' length for a while longer. "Last night?" she whispered.

He smiled, if such an expression could be called a smile. His eyes did not change at all. "Quite delightful," he said. "I compliment you, ma'am. Your eagerness would put a barmaid to shame. You certainly helped pass what would have been a dull night."

Anne said no more. A terrible lethargy was paralyzing her brain and rooting her to the spot.

"You need not worry," Merrick said briskly, moving away from the fireplace across to a large desk in front of the window, from which he picked up a sheaf of papers. "I have spent an hour making arrangements for you here. Your needs will be amply provided for. You will find the servants loyal and eager to please. I shall make you an allowance that I believe you will find ample. If you need more money, you have only to send the bills to me. I shall pay them, provided they are kept within reasonable limits. You will be delighted to learn that you have married a wealthy man, ma'am."

"I shall go back to Bruce," Anne said quietly. "You need not be concerned with me, my lord."

"On the contrary," he said, "I have every need. You are my wife and I shall take care of your needs. I forbid you to leave this estate for so much as a single night without my personal permission. Is that clearly understood?"

Anne did not look up at him. She was examining the backs of her hands. "Yes," she whispered.

"I shall bid you good morning, then," Merrick said, hesitating only a brief moment before striding from the room.

Anne saw him again only as he rode away alone on the high seat of a curricle. She was standing at the window of the morning room, which she had not left since he had said his farewell.

PART TWO

March and April, 1816

5 It was a bright spring morning. The library windows were wide open to admit the crisp fresh air and the smell of daffodils and new foliage. Outside, the sun shone from a brilliant blue sky onto a new and shining world below. The woods to the west of the house were in bright-green leaf, and the grass beneath them was painted with snowdrops, primroses, and early bluebells. The formal gardens that stretched before the house had been freshly raked, clipped, and mown even though the flowers had not yet bloomed. The new marble fountain at its center spouted clear water from the mouth of a fat cherub.

Inside the library, a slim young lady sat at a delicately carved escritoire, writing paper and pens spread out before her. But she was not writing; she was reading a letter, a slight crease on her brow. She suited her surroundings admirably. A vase of daffodils stood beside her and complemented the primrose color of her light muslin day dress. Her light-brown hair was fashionably dressed, curling softly about her face, tied high at the back, with ringlets clustering against her head and neck. Her heart-shaped face rested on one slim hand as she read, a rather wistful look in her large gray eyes:

You really must come, my dear. I shall not take no for an answer. Unless every member of the family is present for our fiftieth wedding anniversary, both His Grace and I will consider the occasion quite a failure. And you are very definitely a member of the family, though we have not yet met you. It will not do at all, you know, to say that your husband will not permit you to come. I have never heard such nonsense in my life. You must learn from me, my dear, that men sometimes need quite firm handling. You must never let them think that they can control your every movement, or they will become insufferably dictatorial.

Of course, if he has expressly forbidden you to come, you are in a somewhat awkward position. Let me put the matter this way. His Grace is the head of this family. That means that his word is law to all the other members, your husband included. And His Grace has this moment declared in his most forceful ducal manner that I am to say he commands you to come. You have no choice, you see. You must obey a higher authority than your husband. And His Grace added that he will send our own best traveling carriage to bring you. You cannot possibly refuse such an offer. He is most possessive of all his conveyances. You cannot know what an honor he does you. You are to come two days before anyone else is due to arrive so that we will have an opportunity to get to know our granddaughter. It strikes me as a great absurdity that you have held that position for well over a year, yet we have still not had the pleasure of your acquaintance.

Do not fret your mind over Alex, my dear. You may leave him to His Grace and me. Sometimes he needs a severe set-down; he is too stubborn by half. He will not be able to scold you when he knows that you were ordered to come here by His Grace himself. Alex was always a little in awe of his grandfather.

The letter went on to make very definite arrangements of dates and times. Although it was only paper she held in her hand, Anne Stewart felt as if she were in the presence of a very powerful will. She had received the first invitation almost a month before to spend two weeks at Portland House with the rest of the family of the duke and duchess to celebrate their fiftieth wedding anniversary. She had not known what to do on that occasion. She had wanted to go; the letter from the duchess had sounded so friendly. She had written to her husband to ask if she might accept the invitation. His answer had been swift and bluntly in the negative.

However, it appeared now that the duchess was not prepared to accept her refusal. And she had put Anne in a very awkward position. She could not disobey her husband. Although she had not seen him since the morning after their wedding well over a year before, she had always obeyed his final command. Yet she could not disobey the Duke of Portland, either. He was the head of the family into which she had married.

She put the duchess's letter down on the escritoire and crossed to the window. It was so lovely outside. There were the spring flowers growing wild in the grass among the trees. And the daffodils were growing almost as wild beneath the window. The gardener had asked her if he should thin them out, and if he should try to cut back the wild growth at the edge of the wood, where it could be seen from the house. But she had said no to both suggestions. It was the flowers that had kept her sane the year before, she would swear until her dying day. Perhaps they did not quite fit the image of formal beauty that she had had created down the long stretch of land before the house, but that did not matter. The grounds were large enough to allow for great variety.

The formal gardens were one of her great triumphs. When she had finally pulled herself free from the dismals that had engulfed her through those long

winter months after Alexander had so cruelly abandoned her, her thoughts had turned toward improving the house and the estate. And she had begun
with the garden, planning eagerly with the gardener
what might be done, summoning, on his advice, a
well-known landscape artist from London to come
and draw up plans. The fountain had been his idea,
but she had chosen the design, and that cherub that
looked so much like the child she would like to have
had.

The improvements had taken all summer to complete, and had been costly, but they had been worth
every moment and every penny, Anne reflected with
a smile. The house now looked stately and quite
lovely as one approached it up the curved drive
lined with elm trees. And to her, alone in the house
much of the time, the garden had afforded hours of
pleasure. She had written her husband to ask permission to make the improvements, and he had made
no objection. Even when the bills began pouring in,
rather heavier than she had expected, he had made
no comment, but presumably had paid them all. In
fact, she had found her husband to be quite indul-
gent. He had never refused her anything, except
once a visit to London to stay with Sonia for a week,
and now a visit to his grandparents. Of course, he
had always refused her his company, though she had
never asked for it.

She dearly wanted to go. It would be a nerve-racking
experience, of course. The duchess made it appear
as if all members of the family were to be there, and
the house party was to last for two weeks. Anne's
shyness made her cringe at the thought of having to
meet all those people and to socialize with them for
many days. And the duchess seemed a formidable
character, the sort of personality against which Anne's
might crumble altogether. The duke sounded like a
veritable tyrant. But, despite all these facts, they were
all her family. They were people she had every right
to know. And Anne had always felt the absence of

family. Her father had never had much contact with his relatives, and her mother's had withdrawn from their life on her death. She had never felt any particular happiness in the company of either Papa or Bruce. The idea of joining a large family group and knowing that she belonged was an attractive one.

The big problem, of course, was that if the whole family was to be present for the occasion, Alexander would be one of their number. She would see him again. She would be terrified of facing him, knowing that she had disobeyed him in being there. And she had vivid, nightmare memories of that last interview she had had with him, when he had been so cold and unyielding, so devoid of all human sympathy. She recalled with a shiver the distaste and scorn for her that he had not tried to hide from his face or his voice. It had taken her a long time to recover any sort of self-esteem after that experience. He had made her feel utterly ugly and worthless. Should she willingly open herself to another such attack? Would the duchess's assurance that she would explain the situation to him save her from his wrath?

But she had to admit to herself that it was the near certainty of Alexander's presence at Portland House that was really attracting her most. She had tried so hard to hate him; indeed, she did hate him. It was hard to excuse or forgive anyone who could treat a fellow human being with such contempt and cruelty. Yet she had never been able to fall out of love with him. She had relived so many times that first meeting, when he had been so charming, and their wedding night, when he had taught her physical passion and fulfillment, that she was no longer sure what was truth and what was fantasy. Was he really as handsome as she remembered? After he had been gone a few days, she had found that she could see clearly in her mind everything about him except his face. And, as time went on, his whole image blurred, so that she could no longer be sure of anything.

But much as she hated and feared her husband,

Anne longed to see him again. She knew from Sonia, who had spent a week with her the summer before, that he really was handsome and charming and that many women found him attractive. She had learned about the betrothal that he had been about to make when he had married her, and the knowledge had helped explain his bitterness on that occasion. Sonia had finally revealed to her, apparently with great reluctance, that he had a mistress, a married lady of great beauty and wit. But all she knew about him from her own experience was the little she had learned during the few brief days of their acquaintance. She had not even known his given name until it was mentioned during their wedding ceremony. She had never used the name to him. There had been a few letters, all of them in answer to ones she had written, and all of them short and to the point. There was never a word of a personal nature. Even so, those letters had always been housed beneath the pillow of her bed for many nights.

Did she dare? she wondered. Did she dare defy him and go to Portland House, where they would be forced into each other's company for two whole weeks? Would he humiliate her by sending her home again immediately if she did? Would he arrive with his mistress and create for her a hopelessly embarrassing situation? But she did not think she need fear any of these things. Surely the duke would not allow her to be sent home in disgrace. And surely Alexander would not do anything as distasteful as to bring his mistress to his grandparents' home. She would surely be safe from total humiliation.

But how would she behave when confronted with him again? She had dreamed of such a meeting for so long. Was he still laboring under that ridiculous idea he had had that she had somehow lured him into marriage? Almost as if she had seen him coming along the highway and had arranged for the storm to strand him with her. And would he hate her as much if he could see her now? She knew that she was changed from what she had been when he last saw her. The weight had gone first. It had not been a deliberate loss at the start. Her clothes were hanging about her, and Mrs. Rush was clucking her concern before Anne had known that she had lost any weight at all. Misery is a fine enforcer of diets, she had discovered.

When spring had come and she had turned almost defiantly to improving the surroundings in which she seemed doomed to live for the rest of her life, she had also turned her attention to herself. She was slim but haggard, terribly dressed in clothes that would have been unappealing even if they had fit. Her hair had been allowed to grow thick and styleless. It was lifeless and dull. It was at that point that she had discovered what a gem of a maid she had in Bella. The girl had an eye for color and design, and clever hands for arranging. Equally important, perhaps, she had a cousin who was a ladies' maid in a noble house in London. From this cousin she received frequent letters, full of information about the latest styles in clothes and hairstyles.

All Bella needed was a willing victim on whom to practice these new ideas. When she realized that her mistress was becoming dissatisfied with the appearance that the girl had long deplored, she set to work. A creative and eager little seamstress from the neighboring village became a willing accomplice, and soon Anne had as fashionable a wardrobe as many a lady in town, and as stylish a hairdo as any. Bella was extremely proud of her creation and took to scolding her lady if the latter became too interested in Cook's best teatime delights, or if she became so engrossed in her garden that she allowed the wind its will on her complexion and uncovered hair.

If Anne did not quite trust the opinion of her looking glass, she had to believe the praise of Bella, who was just as willing to hand out scoldings, and of Sonia, who had enthusiastically given it as her opinion that marriage must agree with her friend, until she learned the true state of affairs. And there were those looks that she frequently intercepted at church on Sundays, looks from neighboring gentry and from the occasional visitor to the area, telling her that she was desirable or at least worthy of a second glance. She felt pretty, more so than she ever had in her life, even including the time when Dennis was alive.

Was it wise to deliberately seek out Alexander again and risk having her new confidence in herself dashed? He could do it with one sneer. On the other hand, if she could surprise only one look of appreciation or admiration from him, her image of herself would be complete.

Anne wandered back to the escritoire and looked down at the blank paper that lay there. She would accept. She might as well sit down and write to the duchess immediately. She knew deep down that however long she pondered the problem, she would end up going. How could she resist? Alexander would never come to her. That much had become obvious to her a long time before. And she would probably never have the chance again of provoking a meeting with him. It might be very unwise to do so, but the opportunity was quite irresistible. Anyway, she thought, she had the feeling that the duchess really would not accept a refusal. That carriage would come whether she said it might or not, except that if she said no, it might very well contain a very irate duke when it did arrive. He might prove to be just as frightening an adversary as Alexander.

Anne sat and began to write fast, her head bent to the task.

Alexander Stewart, Viscount Merrick, rode his favorite horse to his grandparents' home. It was a beautiful spring day, and Portland House was a mere thirty miles south of London. He left his valet to follow after with a carriage and his trunks.

He was looking forward to the two-week holiday. It was a long time since he had spent more than a single night with his grandparents. Yet to him they were like parents. They had brought him up. Their house seemed more like home to him than his own because that was where he had spent his childhood and his boyhood until he went away to school. Even then, it was to Portland House he had gone during vacations.

He had a great fondness for the two old people. The duke sometimes fooled people who did not know him into thinking that he was some kind of ogre. He certainly looked the part: extremely tall and stout, with florid complexion and steely gray eyes. His coughs and wheezes could easily be mistaken for bellows of rage. And the duchess abetted this image by constantly referring to her husband's commands and pronouncements, as if only she stood between the listener and his wrath. But Merrick knew by experience that a milder man than his grandfather did not exist, but that it was his grandmother who ruled the household and the family with an iron hand. Yet hers was a benevolent rule. Though tyrannical by nature, she had the interests of her family at heart.

It was this fact that had caused Merrick to keep her at arms' length during the last while. She did not approve of the direction his life had taken and she made no scruples about saying so. She had, as he expected, been loudly horrified by the news of his precipitate marriage, and quite irate at his weakness in giving in to the persuasions of a mere country gentleman. She was even more enraged to learn— there had been no keeping it from her—that before abandoning his bride, her grandson had been foolish enough to consummate the marriage. She had refused to talk to him any more during that visit he had made a few days after his wedding.

Yet only a week or so later, the duchess had appeared at his London residence, the duke in tow, demanding to know where his wife was, how long he planned to keep her incarcerated in the country, and

when he planned to present her to them. It had
been very difficult to remain firm against her persuasions. She had argued that since his marriage was
an accomplished fact, he must make the best of it.
The girl must be presented to society; she must be
given a chance to acquire some town bronze. She
must begin producing his heirs.

But Merrick had stood firm and the duchess had
finally gone home, beaten for one of the few times in
her life. At least, he had assumed that she had accepted defeat. But it seemed not. He had been completely surprised to receive a letter from his wife a
few weeks previously to ask if she might accept an
invitation to the house party that was being held in
honor of the fiftieth wedding anniversary of his grandparents. Sly old Grandmamma! He had had to write
back to refuse his permission, feeling himself the
tyrant, as usual.

Merrick frowned and pulled his horse out into the
middle of the road, so that he might pass a farmer's
wagon loaded with hay, which swung precariously
from side to side in front of him. Why did he have to
think of Anne and spoil the lighthearted mood that
the day and his destination had brought on him?
The trouble was that she so often ruined his mood.
He just could not put her out of his mind, and the
more time passed, the more he thought of her.

It was terrible enough to know that one had done
wrong, but it was even worse to know that one had
been too lazy or too cowardly or too something to do
anything to put the situation right again. The trouble with guilt was that it had the tendency to fester
and grow. And the longer one put off the moment
of restitution, the harder it became to do anything.
He had known soon after leaving his wife at Redlands, perhaps even before leaving, that his suspicions and accusations were unjust. He had gone over
almost word for word their first meeting and had
admitted that she had made no deliberate attempt to
deceive him into thinking that she was a servant.

And in light of her real identity, he could see that her manner had not been flirtatious at all.

This knowledge had not done much during those first few days after his return to London to soothe his frustration and his bitterness at the changes in his life, but it had made him feel guilt at the way he had treated an innocent young woman. He had made no attempt at all to make her feel at her ease after their wedding, when he was taking her away from her brother and all she had ever known as home. He had treated her on their wedding night as he would a light-skirts, without any regard for her tender sensibilities. Even though she had seemed to enjoy the experience, he had been wrong to treat her so. And then there had been those brutal words he had spoken before leaving. It would have been better far to have left before she had risen from bed.

He had known all this very soon after leaving her, and he had felt the necessity of apologizing, of doing something to make her life more livable than it could be in that bleak and shabby place that he could never quite think of as home. The trouble at first was that he could not face seeing her again. He remembered the plump figure, the round and childish face, the plain features, the lifeless hair, the apparent lack of personality. The fact that he had found her unexpectedly exciting in bed he had conveniently forgotten. He could not—he would not—live with her as his wife. So he had put off the moment of doing something for her. He would go down to Redlands in the spring, he had promised himself at first. Then it was to be during the summer, when the Season was over. When summer had drawn to a close, he had admitted to himself that he was too embarrassed to make the journey. The moment had passed.

He had tried in small ways to salve his conscience. Whenever she wrote to him to ask for something— once, he gathered, it was some flowers, and another time something else for the garden—he would immediately write to assure her that she could continue

with her plans. Sometimes he wished that she might
demand more so that he could give more. But he
became more and more incapable of meeting her.
He had spent a sleepless night a few months before
after denying her the chance to visit a friend of hers
for a week. He would have been only too glad to let
her go if the friend had lived anywhere but in London. But how could he let her come to the capital,
where he would risk the embarrassment of meeting
her and where it would quickly become known that
the Viscountess Merrick was in town but not at her
husband's residence?

Merrick eased his horse to a walk as a country inn
came into view just ahead. He dismounted and turned
his mount over to an ostler while he entered the
taproom and ordered a mug of ale. The taproom
was empty. It was obviously too early in the day for
the local people to be relaxing in the inn, and it was
not the sort of place where carriages would often
stop. He exchanged pleasantries and comments on
the weather with the innkeeper and moved into the
chimney corner with his ale.

He almost wished now that he had told Anne that
she might accept his grandmother's invitation. It might
have proved a good opportunity to meet her again
and to settle her into a more desirable way of life.
The presence of all the other members of the family
was one fact that had made him react so negatively
when he had first read her letter. He had not wanted
the whole tribe to witness the awkwardness of their
meeting. But now, on second thoughts, he wondered
if the presence of other people would not rather
have eased the tension and helped them to commu-
nicate as sensible adults.

It was too late, anyway. He had said a very positive
no, and she had not written again to argue the point.
It was just as well. It would be very depressing to
have to spend two weeks in the company of such a
dull creature, being civil to her for the sake of ap-
pearances. He would enjoy these two weeks for what

they were worth, catch up on the news of all the cousins and uncles and aunts, resist any attempts on the part of Grandmamma to order his life, and then return to face the Season that would soon be in full swing. He would have Eleanor to help keep him from brooding. It really was most satisfactory to have a married woman as mistress. She offered everything he could desire in company and sensual gratification without any of the demands on his time and emotions that he had found so wearing with other women. Lorraine would probably be back by the time he returned, too. Her honeymoon would be over. But he had to admit to himself that he had felt no more than a pang of nostalgia when he had read her betrothal announcement in the *Gazette*.

Merrick put the empty mug down on the stone hearth and got to his feet. His horse had been fed and watered and was waiting for him at the door when he went outside. He swung himself into the saddle and was on his way again. Perhaps he would pay his wife a visit during the summer. He really should look over the estate in person again, anyway.

6 Freddie Lynwood arrived a day early, much to the annoyance of the Duchess of Portland. But as she said to Anne when her grandson finally allowed himself to be led up to his bedchamber after three cups of tea, five cucumber sandwiches, and four currant cakes, she might have expected as much. Dear Freddie did not have as many wits in his attic as might be deemed his fair share, and as a result, he had developed a keen sense of anxiety. He knew that he was forgetful and that his brain frequently became addled. Consequently, he kept important appointments as soon as he remembered them, and honored invitations in the same way. One of her favorite stories was of his arriving at a London home for a ball, only to find that the family were on their way out to the theater. The ball was scheduled for two days hence. Freddie had been quite undaunted, but had announced that he would stay.

"Only forget if I go back home," he had said. "Won't mind if I make m'self comfortable, will you? Don't need to put yourselves out on my account. Will send home for a change of clothes. Don't let me stop you going to the play."

And he had bowed them off the premises with punctilious courtesy and proceeded to make himself comfortable in the best chair in the drawing room, clad all in lace and silks. He had made himself indispensable on the day of the ball, balanced at the top of a ladder held by two footmen, fitting dozens of new candles into the chandeliers.

The duchess chuckled as she finished the story. "I must confess, though," she said, "that it is far more diverting to have such a thing happen to someone else than it is to have one's own plans thrown into upheaval. I had wanted to spend the whole of today getting to know you, my dear. You were so tired after your journey last night that the evening was quite wasted."

Anne smiled and sipped on her own second cup of tea. "But I have greatly enjoyed today, Your Grace," she said. "I thank you so much for spending time showing me the house. I had no idea that such a magnificent mansion existed outside the pages of a book. And the gardens are lovely. The rose arbor, in particular, has given me ideas for Redlands. I love the gardens there, but they are very open. They need a more secluded area where one can sit quietly during the afternoon."

The duchess rested her chin in the palm of her hand and regarded Anne steadily. "You are very different from what I expected, my dear," she said. "I must confess that my motive for inviting you here two days before the rest of the family was only partly to get to know you. I also planned to use the extra time to try to make you more fashionable. I assumed that after so long in the country, your appearance would be sadly out of date. I was mistaken, I see. And about other things, too."

"I have Bella to thank for my appearance," Anne said. "She scolds and bullies me until I allow her to style my hair and design my clothes according to her directions."

"And very glad I am to hear it," the duchess said. "I really cannot think what Alex has been about all this time. I shall have to have a good talk with him. Better still, I shall turn His Grace loose on him."

Anne's face lost its smile. "Please do not, Your Grace," she said. "He will be angry enough that I am here. I would not wish him to think that I have been complaining to you. Indeed, he has been quite a generous husband."

"Balderdash!" the duchess said. "The boy needs a good set-down. And call me Grandmamma, child."

Anne was much in awe of the duke. She had met him the night before in the drawing room soon after her arrival. He had sat in his chair by the fire, a great mountain of a man, his legs set apart, a large hand spread on each knee. His great neck had bulged over his neckcloth, and bushy eyebrows of a surprisingly dark shade of brown had jutted over sharp eyes. He had coughed and wheezed all the time she had been there, until the duchess had released her by announcing that she must be tired and should retire to bed. But he had said nothing after his first apology for not getting up.

"It's my gout," he had said, glaring at her fiercely, as if she were directly responsible for the state of his health.

She had taken an instant liking to the duchess, a diminutive bundle of energy who appeared to rule her household with a rod of iron. Perhaps the liking came because the duchess was everything she was not, Anne thought. She had perfect self-confidence. And she had done her best to welcome the estranged wife of her grandson. She had herself taken Anne to her room the night before, where Bella had already unpacked her belongings and turned down the bed. And she had hardly left her side during this day, but had shown Anne almost every room in the house, pointing out the remaining signs of the original Tudor manor, most noticeable in the high wooden beams of the dining-room ceiling, as well as the most recent additions, such as the grand marble chimneypiece in one of the state rooms.

Anne had particularly enjoyed the visit to the picture gallery, where were displayed portraits of the

Stewart family for generations back. She listened attentively to all the names and relationships, realizing only then how strange her situation was. She had been married for well over a year, yet she knew almost nothing of her husband's family. It had been a very difficult moment, though, when they had stopped before Alexander's portrait. It had been a long time since Anne had been able to remember clearly what he looked like. She retained only a general memory of height and athletic build, of dark hair and blue eyes and overall beauty. Her heart seemed to stop altogether as she looked on him once more and then started again with a painful thud. Yes, of course, that was he. How could she ever have forgotten? She could not linger as she would have wished because the duchess chattered at her side and proceeded to the next picture almost immediately.

The newly arrived member of the family had won Anne's heart almost immediately. She did not share the duchess's annoyance at his early arrival. When Freddie had been introduced to her, he had bowed over her hand with courtly grace and kissed it.

"Alex's wife?" he had said, brows knit in concentration. "When did he tie the knot? Don't remember to have met you before. But, damme, yes, if I didn't hear something of the kind from Jack. Now what did he say?" Freddie had retained his hold on Anne's hand while the frown on his face indicated that he was deep in slow thought. "Damme if I can remember," he had said, "but whatever it was, he was dead wrong. Dead wrong," he had repeated, wringing her hand until she thought she would have to bite her lip from the pain of it.

"Your hand, Freddie," the duchess had said bluntly. "It belongs at your side, dear boy."

"Forgot," he had said, smiling affably at Anne. "I like you. Damme if Alex hasn't done an intelligent thing. Always was intelligent, you know, Alex. A real sharper. Saw him read a book once. Didn't even

have to move his lips. I might have a wife like you,
you know, if I had some of Alex's brains. Lucky
dog." He had flashed her a smile of boyish charm.

"Your hand, Freddie," the duchess had reminded
him, and finally he had relinquished his hold on Anne.

If only the other members of the family could be
as unthreatening to her self-confidence as Freddie,
Anne thought, she would endure any number of
painful finger squeezes. But she spent an uncomfortable portion of that night wondering if she had
done a foolish thing in coming to face them all in
one splash. There would be no backing out of the
ordeal, either. Tomorrow they would all arrive—a
large number of them, to judge from the duchess's
conversation today—and she would be forced to meet
them and mingle with them for two whole weeks.

That, of course, was not her only, or even her
chief, worry. Tomorrow Alexander would come. She
would see him again. She would know him, at least;
her sight of his portrait that afternoon had ensured
that. But she did not know at all how she would
behave. Would she be able to retain her poise, or
would she blush and stammer and lose all control of
her reactions? She did not know. And she did not
know how many other people would be present during that meeting. It could all prove to be a great
embarrassment both to her and to him.

Most of all, Anne was afraid of his reaction. He
did not know that she would be here. She had not
written to tell him that she had accepted the invitation. She had been too afraid that he would again
send instructions forbidding her to do so. She was, if
she really paused to admit the truth, feeling sick with
fear. She had disobeyed one of his express commands. And it was no private matter, which he could
have dealt with in his own way. She had flouted his
authority before his whole family. She dreaded to
imagine what he might say to her or what he might
do. Perhaps she was foolish to worry about having to
mingle with the guests for two weeks. This time

tomorrow night she might well be on her way back to Redlands. But no! She reminded herself that the duke would surely not allow any such thing. It was at his direct bidding that she was here, and he was the head of the family.

When Merrick arrived at Portland House, it was already late afternoon, and he could see at a glance that several members of his family must be there before him. The huge double doors of the main entrance stood open, and several liveried footmen were busily carrying inside large trunks and boxes that had just been unloaded from an ancient traveling carriage that still stood before the entry. Some female was in the rose arbor: probably his second cousin Constance. She looked too fair and too small to be the older sister, Prudence. Freddie Lynwood was outside among the boxes, looking quite painful to the eye with a large expanse of canary-yellow waistcoat showing beneath an unbuttoned coat. He was good-naturedly trying to help the footman by gathering three bandboxes into his arms.

Jack Frazer was also outside, and obviously newly arrived. He stood with one shoulder indolently propped against the side of the carriage, one Hessian boot crossed over the other, a whip swinging idly from his hands. He grinned when he saw Merrick.

"You must have been riding in our dust, Alex," he said. "I have just succeeded in conveying Mamma and Hortie safely here, though Mamma must have had thirty fits of the vapors on the way, so convinced was she that we would be attacked by highwaymen. It is a good thing for you, old boy, that you did not come up on us a little sooner. I might have been forced to shoot you just to put her mind at rest."

"I should not have enjoyed that at all," Merrick commented dryly as he swung himself to the ground and patted his horse's flank.

"I see, at any rate, that you were as little able to come up with a previous engagement for these two weeks as I was," Jack said, still grinning. "Grand-mamma is not to be denied when she has her heart set on something, is she?"

"Ah, but then I was not looking for an excuse," Merrick said, nodding a greeting to Freddie, who had set down his bandboxes at the top of the stone steps leading to the door, not knowing where he was to take them. "You look as if you are thoroughly settled in, Freddie. I suppose you arrived a few days ago?"

"Hello, Alex," Freddie said, beaming. "Arrived yesterday. Thought I would be late. Expected to see Grandmamma in a lather. But was a day early. She was pleased to see me, though. No other man except Grandpapa to keep the ladies company."

Merrick's attention was taken at that moment by the arrival on the scene of the duchess. She descended the steps and extended both hands to Jack, who pulled himself upright at her approach.

"Jack," she said, "you are just as handsome as ever, I see. And still breaking female hearts by the dozen, I should not wonder. Do go inside and join your sister and your mamma for refreshments in the blue salon. Stanley and Celia are there, too. They arrived more than an hour ago, but they had to take their children up to the nursery and could not get away. They did not bring their own nurse, you know, and the little devils have been throwing tantrums every time their mamma tries to leave the room. However, all seems quiet now."

"Grandmamma," Jack said, kissing dutifully the cheek that was offered him, "how can this possibly be your fiftieth anniversary? You do not look a day over fifty yourself. You must have been an infant bride."

"Shameless flatterer!" she said. "Go inside immediately, and take Freddie with you so that the servants can get something done out here."

She turned to Merrick when the other two men finally disappeared indoors. "Alex," she said, "it is about time you put in an appearance, dear boy. You have become quite the stranger." She offered him, too, her cheek, but he ignored it and caught her around the waist, lifting her from her feet and twirling her completely around. She shrieked. "Put me down immediately," she ordered. "Have you completely lost your wits?"

Merrick grinned. "Grandmamma," he said, "if you intend to scold for the next two weeks, I shall mount this horse and turn its head for London again. Am I not going to be offered tea with the Frazers and Stanley and Celia?"

"In a little while," the duchess said. "First, be a dear boy and go fetch whoever that is in the rose arbor."

Merrick turned his eyes in the direction of the distant female again. "Who is she, anyway?" he asked. "Constance?"

"Oh, go see, dear boy," she said vaguely, beginning to waft her way back to the house. "I have a thousand and one things on my mind."

"What a greeting!" Merrick said with a grin, handing the reins of his horse to a waiting groom, and his hat and greatcoat to a footman who happened to pass with a free hand.

He strode toward the rose arbor, which was still looking pretty bare at this time of the year, he noted. But there was certainly something to add attraction to the area. She had her back to him, her fair head, clustered with curls at the back, bent over a book. She was seated on a bench, one leg crossed over the other, a rose-pink slipper swinging from side to side beneath the hem of a matching dress. She had a white lace shawl over her shoulders.

Merrick was intrigued. It was true that he had not seen some of his cousins for quite some time, but he had thought that he would recognize them. It was hard, he supposed, to remember that those girls he had known from infancy had grown into young ladies, and possibly attractive ones at that. This one was very attractive, if one might judge from behind.

She turned as he stooped to pass through the trellised arch that formed the entryway to the arbor, and he realized that she was not one of his cousins. Grandmamma had said nothing about inviting anyone from outside the family, and he was momentarily annoyed that she had not told him who the girl was. On second thoughts, he blessed his good fortune that he could meet her thus in private. She was an exquisite little beauty—and a shy one too, if one might judge by the color that suffused her cheeks and the urge that caused her to leap to her feet and drop her book.

He smiled, stepped forward, and retrieved the volume. "Jane Austen," he said, glancing at the title. "Do you enjoy her works?"

"I have read only *Mansfield Park*," she said in a tight little voice.

He tapped the book against his other hand as he examined her. She was a light little creature with a good figure. And she was pretty too, her heart-shaped face made appealing by hollowed cheeks, high cheekbones, and large gray eyes that looked at him now anxiously, almost fearfully. She was not as young as he had at first thought. Her face had character. He was aware finally that the silence was lengthening between them.

"Alex Stewart," he said, holding out his right hand, "the duke's grandson." He raised his eyebrows inquiringly.

Heaven help her, he had not recognized her. At first she had thought that the duchess had sent him to her and that he had decided to be fair and friendly about the whole business. She had been sitting here for longer than half an hour, reading and rereading the same paragraph without absorbing any of its meaning, wondering when he would come and what would happen when he did. The duchess had sent her after she had taken tea with two batches of newly arrived family members. But he had not been sent. He did not know her. Alexander. So much more powerfully attractive than she remembered.

"Alexander," she said, not taking the proffered hand, "do you not know me?"

He frowned and looked at her closely for several seconds. His face noticeably paled as his hand dropped to his side. "My God," he said, "who are you?"

She grasped the sides of her dress and twisted the fabric in her hands. His eyes followed the gesture.

"Anne," he said. His eyes lifted to hers, and his own suddenly blazed. "Anne? What is the meaning of this, madam? By what right have you dared present yourself here?"

"Don't be angry," she said. "Grandpapa insisted that I come. Indeed, I wrote to Grandmamma to explain that you did not wish it, but she wrote back to say that His Grace is head of the family and I must obey him."

"I am your husband, madam," he said. "It is to me—and to me alone—that you owe obedience. And by what right do you call the Duke and Duchess of Portland by such familiar names?"

"The duchess has insisted that I do so," Anne said, tears standing in her eyes. "Please, Alexander, do not be angry. I shall try not to bother you in the coming days. You need not know that I am here."

"Need not know!" he said. "How will I be able to avoid the knowledge, madam? You have the advantage of me. I have been taken quite by surprise. And I have been sent to bring you in for tea. Come. Allow me to escort you. But do not think that you have escaped lightly. I shall consider later how to deal with your disobedience." Unsmilingly, his face pale and set, Merrick transferred the book to his right hand and held out his left arm for her support.

Anne took his arm, her eyes lowered. She did not want him to see the tears that were about to spill down her cheeks. But she feared that he would feel her trembling. Indeed, she was glad that she was not called upon to speak. Her jaw was tightly clenched to prevent her teeth from chattering. The combination of his anger and his physical nearness and touch was more than her fragile self-confidence could handle at present.

There followed a tricky half-hour. Anne seated herself behind the teapot and tried to be unobtrusive, but there were a few newcomers, who had arrived since she had been sent to the rose arbor. One young man closely resembled her husband, except that he was somewhat thinner and had the tendency to view the world with amused eyes from beneath lazy eyelids. He immediately got to his feet when he saw a stranger.

"Well, well," he said, "it looks as if Grandmamma has arranged for some interesting company, after all. It is just like you, Alex, to be the first to find her. You must not think that gives you undisputed rights to her company for the next two weeks, though. Introduce me, old boy." He strolled across to the table where Anne sat, and leered down at her.

Merrick had dissociated himself from his wife as soon as they entered the blue salon and had crossed the room to greet his father's nephew, Stanley. He turned back to face the room, his face still pale and grim. "May I present my wife, Anne?" he said, looking around at all the occupants. "Have you met everyone, Anne, and had the relationships explained to you. Aunt Maud Frazer and Aunt Sarah Lynwood are my father's sisters. Jack and Hortense are Aunt Maud's offspring. Uncle Charles and Cousin Freddie belong to Aunt Sarah. Stanley and Celia Stewart are the son and daughter-in-law of Grandpapa's youngest brother. Still upstairs are Grandmamma's sister, Great-aunt Emily, and her family." Merrick had indicated each member of the family as he spoke.

"Charles and I met Anne earlier," Aunt Sarah said with a smile, "and so did Aunt Emily and her brood. I don't know what keeps them abovestairs so long. Is she holding a family conference up there, Mamma?"

Jack still stood opposite Anne, regarding her with that strange, amused scrutiny. "Well, well," he said, for her ears only, "the abandoned bride. I had expected to see a veritable antidote. Has Alex been afraid to take you to town for fear that someone else would run off with you?" He grinned as Anne kept her eyes on the table and straightened plates and linen napkins that did not need rearranging. "I shall look forward to making your acquaintance, Anne," he said. "If Alex has no interest in you, perhaps I can deputize for him."

"Did you want more tea, Jack?" Merrick asked, moving up to stand beside his cousin. "If so, I am sure my wife would be very willing to pour it for you."

Jack grinned. "You should know, Alex," he said, "that tea is not quite my cup of tea, so to speak. Is one permitted to speak to your wife, old boy, without incurring your wrath?"

Merrick smiled easily back at him. "Not when he causes her such noticeable embarrassment," he replied.

Jack sighed. "I perceive that there is to be little fun connected with this celebration," he said.

The duchess's voice had risen in volume, indicating that she was about to make a general pronouncement. "His Grace has decided," she said, resting a hand lightly on the arm of her husband, who had sat silent and frowning through the whole tea, "that we must have some activity to give focus to these two weeks. We both remember how years ago, when many of you were children, you all used to love the plays we performed for the servants at Christmas. Amateur theatrics, His Grace has decided, is just the thing to keep us all pleasantly occupied until the night of the grand ball. We have exactly two weeks to prepare. We shall perform a play for all the guests who have been invited, between the dinner hour and the start of the dancing." She patted the duke's arm again.

"Grandmamma!" Hortense shrieked. "How are we to choose a play, allot parts, learn lines, and produce a polished performance all in two weeks?"

"Impossible!" Stanley agreed.

The duchess held up a hand for attention. "That is where I have taken the initiative," she said. "I have a play already selected and I have decided who is to play which parts. All you have to do, my dears, is to learn and perform your lines."

"Mamma!" Sarah said severely. "We came here to be with you and Papa and to relax."

The duke produced a rumbling sound in his throat, which might have been a cough. "Boredom," he said. "Relaxation produces boredom. This'll keep you all busy."

"Damme if I don't think this a grand idea," Freddie said, smiling eagerly around at the group. "If I just had some brains, I would have a part. No memory, though. Can never remember lines, and when I do, don't know when to say them."

"You have a part too, Freddie, my boy," the duchess assured him.

Freddie giggled.

"What is the play, anyway?" Sarah asked. "Something short, I hope."

"*She Stoops to Conquer*," the duchess said, gazing imperiously around her, daring anyone to complain about the choice. "We shall all meet in the morning room after breakfast tomorrow, and I shall allot parts. There will be no arguments, and I expect everyone to learn his lines."

Jack groaned. "In the absence of any stronger beverage," he said, "I had better fortify myself with more tea. Will you pour, Anne?"

7 The whole family gathered in the morning room the next morning except the duke, who was reported to be nursing his gout in his private apartments. Those who assembled displayed a variety of moods, from enthusiastic (Freddie) to downright belligerent (Jack), but it was a tribute to the power the duchess exerted over her family that all were there and none was openly arguing against the projected dramatic presentation.

"Who knows this play, anyway?" the duchess's nephew, Martin Raine, asked of the room at large, while the duchess sat at a desk and perused a sheaf of notes through her lorgnette. "Is it a comedy or a melodrama or a tragedy or what?"

"We saw it performed last year," Celia offered. "A very comical play. But I fail to see how we are to produce it in just two weeks. We shall doubtless make cakes of ourselves."

"Balderdash!" said the duchess, not raising her eyes from her task.

"Oliver Goldsmith wrote it," Stanley said. "I wonder you have not heard of it, Martin."

"I don't get to town often," Martin replied. "The last thing I saw performed was *The Beggar's Opera.*

And glad I am that Aunt Jemima did not choose that one."

"Yes, I have it all organized now," the duchess said, raising her head and commanding silence with one glance. "Claude," she looked at her sister's second son, "you always took charge of the Christmas theatrics years ago. I am putting you in charge of directing this play. All the rest of you must accept his authority without question." She stared around the group, daring anyone to contradict.

Claude clasped his hands across a somewhat rotund middle and blew a mock sigh of relief. "Well, Aunt Jemima," he said, "I cannot pretend to be wholly thrilled, but at least I can now relax and not be afraid that I will be called upon to act."

The duchess held up her hand for silence. "Let us not waste time," she said. "The sooner you all know the parts you are to play, the sooner you can get busy on learning your lines. And remember that you do not have a great deal of time in which to do so. Now. There are two pairs of lovers in the play, and several character parts, which may not be as large, but which require a deal of good acting. First of all, to set your mind at rest, Freddie, dear boy, I do indeed have a part for you. There are not many lines involved, but you are required to laugh in a few places and to behave in a very confused manner throughout. The character's name is Diggory."

"Diggory," Freddie said. "I'll do it, Grandmamma. Learn my lines night and day. I can laugh, y' know."

"Yes, I do know, dear boy," she said. "The main pair of lovers are Kate Hardcastle and Charles Marlow, who falls in love with her thinking she is the maid of the house when she is really the daughter. A highly unlikely plot, of course, but it is meant to be a comedy. I want Anne to be Kate and Alex to be Marlow."

"No," Merrick said, rising to his feet and then sitting again when he realized that there was nowhere to go. "I know the play, Grandmamma, and

Marlow's is a big part. You know I am far too lazy to learn the half of it."

"Balderdash," she said, raising her lorgnette to her eye and surveying him through it.

"Grandmamma," Anne said timidly from her place on a sofa between the duchess's two young grandnieces, Prudence and Constance Raine, "I have never acted in my life or seen a play, in fact. I beg that you will give the part to someone else and let me observe for this occasion. Perhaps some other time."

"If you are to be a member of this family, my dear," the duchess said kindly but firmly, "you must learn to act. We all do, you know. And there is no time like the present."

Anne sat very still, completely caught up in her own dismay. She heard none of the other announcements or the comments and protests of the other would-be actors. It was not enough, it seemed, that she had mastered her own terrible shyness and come to this house party, where she would meet all her husband's family. And she had been so proud of herself. She had not cringed from any of the introductions and had made an effort to converse with all of them with whom she had come into close contact. But now she was being called upon to act in a play, and the major role, at that. And they were to perform the play before a crowd of the duke's neighbors and several friends who were coming out from London for the anniversary ball. The very thought made her feel faint.

The worst of it was, though, that she would have to act with Alexander. Their characters were lovers, the duchess had said. That would mean that they would be together a great deal on stage and be forced to speak words of love. Perhaps they would even have to touch. Perhaps kiss? Anne did not know what was permitted to happen during a play. She had never seen one. The only time a traveling company of actors had come within visiting distance of their home, Bruce had refused to allow her to go. To him, acting was a creation of the devil.

She could not do it. She really could not, even to please the duchess. How could she look at Alexander and speak words of love to him when she knew that he hated her so much? He had promised her the day before that he would think of a suitable way of punishing her for disobeying his command to stay away. She did not know if he had yet punished her enough. She really did not know if the night before had been the punishment or not.

He had come to her room when she was still brushing her hair before her mirror, clad in her usual linen nightgown, trimmed at neck and wrists with lace. He had not knocked, and she had gaped at his reflection in the mirror, the brush stilled against her hair.

"Alexander," she had said foolishly, "what do you want?"

He had raised his eyebrows and gazed back at her reflection, his expression cynical. "I wonder you ask," he had replied. "You came here of your own free will, madam. I assume that you came here to perform again your wifely duties."

"No," she had said, putting down the brush with a clatter onto the dresser and spinning around to face him, "no, Alexander, please don't. Please."

His cynical look had deepened. "I am devastated, madam," he had said. "Am I to believe that my person is not desirable enough to you? I do not remember any words in the marriage service that said you owed me obedience only as long as you found me attractive."

She had shaken her head and pressed against the hard edge of the dresser. How could she explain to him that her reluctance had nothing to with her feelings for him or her attraction to him. She could not bear to be taken out of contempt and even hatred. That had happened to her once before, and the experience had scarred her for a lifetime, she felt. Certainly she had never quite recovered from the feeling of degradation that had followed upon that night of ecstasy. Not again. Please, not again.

His fingers had threaded their way through her hair until her head was his prisoner. "No," she had said, tears springing to her eyes. "Please, Alexander. Please. Oh, please."

The trouble was, she admitted to herself now, that those pleadings had taken on a double meaning. He had kissed her throat as his hand opened her nightgown down the front, and she had become lost in her own desire for the man she had loved almost from the moment when she had first set eyes on him. Passion had flared in her with shockingly little resistance, and finally she had urged him on, pleading against his hair, against his cheek, and against his mouth.

It had not been a shared experience. She had abandoned herself to the passion that his expertise aroused with such ease. She had clung to him, opened to him, arched herself to his invasion, cried out to him, and shuddered against him at the end of it all. And then she had slept deeply with her cheek against his damp shoulder. But she had not known what had motivated him. He had not been tender, she knew that, but then neither had she. Their lovemaking had been too charged with emotion to allow for that. He had said nothing, not looked into her eyes once while he took her or afterward, and had not held her or touched her when it was over. But neither had he moved away from her touch when she had laid her cheek against his shoulder. And he had slept beside her all through the night, rising and leaving her room only when she awoke and moved her head to look at him. He had looked back, unsmiling, got out of the bed, pulled on his nightshirt and dressing gown without any appearance of embarrassment, and left the room without a word or a backward glance.

"It still seems funny to me that Great-aunt Jemima has given me the part of Constance Neville," Prudence Raine was confiding to Anne, "when I have a sister Constance. It is going to be most confusing. But so exciting. I was secretly hoping that I would have one of the main parts, weren't you, Anne?"

"I am paralyzed by terror," Anne replied. "I shall rely on you to help me learn how to act, Prudence."

She looked across the room to Alexander, who was indulgently listening to an excited monologue by Freddie. Her insides performed a curious somersault. He looked so formal and impersonal dressed still in the riding clothes that he had worn for an early ride. And very, very handsome. Yet this was the man who had used her so intimately just a few hours before. Was the punishment over? Would he come to her again? How could she live if he did not? Her face suffused with color as he raised his head and looked full at her, the smile that had been donned for Freddie's benefit fading completely. He held her look until she turned away jerkily and smiled for no reason at all at Constance Raine, who sat quietly beside her.

Until the middle of the afternoon, one would not have been able to find any privacy in any of the public rooms of Portland House. Claude Raine had taken possession of the drawing room and was reading through the whole play, trying to imagine what he wished it all to look like at the end of the two weeks. He very much feared that reality would in no way match the ideal. How could he bully them all into spending the next two weeks learning lines and practicing scenes, when most of them had come with the idea that they were about to have a holiday? He sighed. Why did none of them have the courage to stand up against Aunt Jemima and tell her they just would not do it? For the same reason that they had never stood up to her within living memory, he supposed. She was just plain overpowering. It was really amusing how she kept alive the myth that it was Uncle Roderick who was really the originator of all her mad ideas.

Prudence returned to the morning room after luncheon and read through the part of Constance Neville. It was a flatteringly big part, and she was excited by the fact that Jack was to be her lover, Hastings. Jack was only a second cousin, of course, but even she could see that he was a very attractive man. Even if she had not noticed, her friends in town would have apprised her of the fact. Jack was a great favorite, especially with the debutantes, with whom he loved to flirt.

Jack himself was in the garden, stretched beneath an oak tree, trying halfheartedly to keep his eyes open and on the book that was on the grass beside him. He might have known that Grandmamma would have the whole thing thoroughly organized. He had hoped for a while that morning that she would have forgotten they could not all learn their lines from one copy of the play. He had looked forward to witnessing her chagrin and disappointment. Of course, when luncheon was over, a footman had brought into the dining room a disconcertingly large pile of books, and they all had a copy, down to the one who had the part of the least maid.

Damn his luck! He leafed through the pages once more to assure himself that he had made no mistake. There were lots of lines. And not even a chance to have fun. Prudence! He had known her since she was in leading strings and found her quite unappealing, even though he was forced to admit that she was passably pretty. Now if only Grandmamma could have paired him with that little wife of Alex's. He certainly fancied her, and he might stand some chance of success, if her husband's attentions to her since their wedding were anything to go on. Jack lost his battle with sleep as he was still musing on the pleasant possibilities.

Freddie sat in the breakfast room, his book propped

open on the table before him. A frown of concentration creased his brow and his lips moved as he mouthed over his part. "Damme," he muttered to himself, "if I will ever remember when to say these lines. Will probably be so nervous that I'll string them all together. Wish I had Alex's brains. Or even Jack's." His face broke into a grin suddenly and he began to giggle as he read about the joke that Mr. Hardcastle told his servants, including Freddie's own character, Diggory, with strict instructions that they were not to laugh at it when he told it again to his guests at the dinner table.

Maud Frazer, Jack's mother, sat in the conservatory, one hand playing absently with an aspidistra leaf as she read through the part of Mrs. Hardcastle. "What a widgeon!" she said aloud. "Whatever possessed Mamma to cast me in this part? This woman is downright silly." She turned back to the beginning of the play, read over her first speech, and raised her eyes to the glass roof above her head, trying to repeat the words to herself.

Martin Raine, brother of Claude, was similarly employed in trying to memorize the opening scene of the play. He wished it was his cousin Sarah rather than his cousin Maud, though, who would be playing Mrs. Hardcastle to his Mr. Hardcastle. He had fancied Sarah years ago when they were both young; he probably would have married her if they had not been first cousins. He had never told her that, of course, but he had always had a soft spot for her, even after she married dull Charles Lynwood and produced that unspeakable oaf Freddie. He had never married. Now, why would Aunt Jemima give him the part of a cosily married man with a grown-up daughter on whom he doted? Sometimes the woman had no sense at all. But who had the nerve to tell her so?

Peregrine Raine, son of Claude and brother of Prudence and Constance, was in the blue salon, lounging inelegantly in a large, comfortable chair. He was grinning and reading with obvious enjoyment. It was clear to him why Great-aunt Jemima had given him the part of Tony Lumpkin. He was the least physically attractive of all the younger members of the family, being somewhat overweight and having had the misfortune to lose most of his hair between his twentieth and his four-and-twentieth year. However, he was not offended. He had always loved the family theatrics. In fact, he was the only family member that he knew of who would have wanted to put on those Christmas plays even without the goading of the duchess. His appearance had always worked to his advantage, as a matter of fact. While the more attractive males—Jack and Alex in particular—had always got the dull leading roles, he was always given the character parts. And this was no exception. He loved the vulgar, riotous character of the childish Tony. He was already imagining in his mind what tune he could use to sing the raucous song that Tony was to sing at the Three Jolly Pigeons alehouse.

The lesser characters were dotted around the house and grounds, blessing their good fortune in being given parts with only a few lines to remember. Not for them the prospect of two weeks of hard work, incarcerated in one of the rooms of Portland House conning lines.

Anne was in the rose arbor. She had read the play through without stopping. It was thoroughly enchanting. There was the humor, of course, which would be its chief appeal to an audience, she felt sure. But the romance of it! How she admired Kate Hardcastle, who had the spirit to defy her father and fight to win the man with whom she had fallen in love, even when his behavior was puzzling and not everything she could have desired. If only she could have been that way with Alexander. Kate would never have meekly allowed him to walk out of her life and then to walk back into it as if he had never been gone. Kate would have given as good as she had received.

But she had a chance to be Kate for two weeks.

And she would be playing opposite Alexander. She would be only acting, of course, but she could also fantasize, pretend that she really was Kate behaving thus to her lover. Everyone would think that she was merely acting. No one would suspect what she was really doing, playacting in earnest. Now that the shock of the duchess's announcement had had a chance to wear off, Anne found within herself a growing excitement. She was going to learn her part so thoroughly that she would not have to think about the words or when she was to say them. Then she would be able to concentrate all her energies on bringing the part alive on the stage. She would be able to concentrate on stooping to conquer Alexander, even if it were only in her imagination.

Merrick was in his room, sitting sideways on the window seat, one leg propped on it, his forearm resting across his raised knee. The air felt delightfully cool through the open window. He would have loved to change into his riding clothes again and take his horse out for a gallop. But he had to stay here and learn this damned part. He might have guessed that Grandmamma would come up with some such harebrained notion. No one in his right mind, of course, would accept the theory that the idea and the command had originated with Grandpapa. No one was fooled by that myth, but she seemed to delight in keeping it alive.

If only she had given him a different part, or given Anne a different part. She really did have a fiendish mind. He had always thought so but had never had such glaring proof as he had now. She knew that they were estranged. She must know that he had been less than pleased to find his wife in residence when he had arrived yesterday. It was all her doing, of course. Grandpapa, left to himself, would have taken a thousand years to conceive the idea of using his position as head of the family to override the command of a man to his wife. She was trying to bring them back together, but her tactics were so obvious that she was like to make them the laughingstock.

Merrick did not have to read the play that lay open before him to the first page. He had seen it performed several times. He had always enjoyed it and would normally have fallen in with the duchess's plans—if not with enthusiasm, at least with willingness. But he would have to flirt with Anne, even to the extent of stealing a kiss, before an audience. He wondered if his grandmother had chosen the play with the fact in mind that the situation between the two main characters resembled to an uncomfortable degree his own first meeting with his wife. In the play, Charles Marlow mistook the daughter of the house for the maid because she was dressed in country style. He attempted to seduce her and discovered the truth only when her father and his own intervened. Merrick ground his teeth. He certainly did not need the play to remind him of how he had acted the fool.

If he leaned slightly forward toward the window, he could see Anne below him, sitting in the rose arbor, reading. Was she, too, realizing the parallels between the play and her own experience? He was going to find it impossible to act with her. All the others would be watching them, wondering about the true state of their marriage. Sometimes he could contemplate horrible tortures for his dear, interfering grandmother.

What was the state of his marriage, anyway? He was still shaken by the change in her. He hated to admit it, but she was quite beautiful now. Had he recognized her immediately the afternoon before, perhaps he could have protected himself from that feeling of powerful attraction that had swept over him. But yet again she had unwittingly put him into the position of feeling very foolish. How could a man speak to his own wife for a whole minute or two without knowing her? His embarrassment had very quickly converted into anger. Perhaps he had been unfair, but she should have revealed herself sooner. Was he always to appear at a disadvantage before her?

Merrick put his head back against the wall behind him. Why had he gone to her last night? It was really a foolish thing to have done. He had resumed the marriage and perhaps given her the argument she needed to be taken back with him when he returned to London after the anniversary ball. It would have been far better to have stayed angry, to have concentrated his mind on that punishment he had promised her. But punishment for what? She had only obeyed a command from an old woman whom even the strongest man had never been able to withstand for as far back as Merrick could remember.

He could not understand his own feelings. He had almost always felt in command of himself where women were concerned. Even when he had been about to betroth himself to Lorraine, he had made a conscious decision, weighing all the advantages of such a match. He always chose his mistresses with care, considering their beauty, social position, tact, and intelligence. He had never allowed himself to be swayed by emotion alone. With Anne he could be sure of nothing. For a long time he had felt guilty, pitying her alone on his run-down estate. He had felt that he should return to her, if only to make her a decent settlement and set her free to choose a more congenial place to live.

Now his mind was totally confused. He had had no willpower the night before to stay away from her. He had hidden his own perplexity behind a mask of cold cynicism, but he had wanted her with an ache that was not to be denied. And as soon as he had touched her, he had been back in their wedding chamber, where he had surprised himself with the strength of his own desire for her. He had blocked that memory from his mind, as it was totally inconsistent with his general feeling of distaste for a bride whom he had seen as dull and almost ugly. But there had been no holding back the memory the night before. She had smelled of the same wholesome soap as she had before, and her body had responded with the same heat and eager surrender. She was undoubtedly, and surprisingly, a woman of great passion. He had completely lost control of his own reactions. He had not been able to make love to her as if he despised her, but had taken her as if she were his very life.

Would he go to her again tonight? And tomorrow night? If he wished to retain any control over his own life, he must stay away. He could not allow himself to be ruled by a little mouse of a woman who somehow always seemed able to make him look foolish.

Damn Grandmamma! Merrick picked up his copy of the play, slammed it closed, and hurled it onto a table that stood a short distance from the window. He felt better for a moment.

8 Three days later tempers were becoming somewhat frayed. Prudence, forgetting her early excitement over being given a big part, grumbled to Anne that Great-Aunt Jemima had gathered them all together under false pretenses. They had been invited to a two-week house party, but instead they had been recruited as a slave gang. All she had wanted was free performers for an entertainment for all her guests on the night of the ball. She could easily have hired a group of players to come and act at the house. She could well afford it. Everyone knew what an old moneybags Great-uncle Roderick was. A girl should be in London already, waiting for the Season to begin in full swing. A girl should be having fun, especially when she was only nineteen years old. It was fine for Constance, maybe. At sixteen, her sister could not expect much social activity. She might well think it fun to be involved in staging a dramatic production. But for everyone else . . .

Jack was loud and indiscriminate in his complaints. Grandmamma had clearly forgotten what it was like to be below the age of forty. Did she really believe that one could derive entertainment from cavorting around a stage all day and all night, bullied and harangued by a dry middle-aged stick who would be satisfied with no less than perfection? It would not be as intolerable, perhaps, if one were not surrounded so exclusively by one's cousins. Hortense was pretty enough, and Prudence had a certain spirit that one might admire. Constance was too young to be noticed, though she promised well. But how could one get excited about females with whom one had romped as a child?

He did not add aloud to anyone that the only female who might have brightened his stay was proving quite elusive. She made life interesting, of course, but one never quite knew where one stood with old Alex. He had married the girl a few years before, Jack gathered, because he had felt he had compromised her in some way, and then he had left her and presumably forgotten her very existence. It was only fair that another fellow should be free to try his luck with her. But Alex had jumped to her defense that first afternoon, and he had a disconcerting habit of turning up at the wrong moment, just as if he were any ordinary jealous husband.

There had been the afternoon before, for example, when Claude had announced that he needed only Maud and Martin for rehearsal. Jack had seen Anne, book in hand, wander off along the tree-lined driveway toward the main gates almost two miles distant. He had been quick to follow and to catch up with her out of sight of the house.

"Anne," he had said, favoring her with the smile that usually brought color to the cheeks of any female, "I see that you too feel the need for air and exercise. Do you mind if I walk with you?"

"Not at all, Jack," she had said in the quiet voice that had come to intrigue him. And he was gratified to note that she had blushed.

He had given her time to get used to his presence, walking silently at her side and looking up into the treetops. "Are you happy to be here?" he had asked. "The grounds are quite splendid, are they not? I imagine it is quite a welcome change for you to be here after living at Redlands for so long. A drab old place, as I remember."

"Oh," she had said, turning to him an animated face, "it is no longer so. I have had an ornamental garden created before the house. It stretches for fully half a mile. It looks lovely even at this time of year with box hedges and lawns and graveled walks and a fountain in the middle of it all. But soon it will be quite glorious. I can hardly wait to get back home so that I might not miss the flowers beginning to bloom."

"Indeed?" he had said quietly, looking steadily at her. "I might have known, Anne, that you would not live there fretting. You are a beautiful little creature who would have to spread beauty around you."

Anne had looked startled and blushed hotly. "Oh," she had said, "what a strange thing to say."

"I should like to see what you have done to the old place," he had said. "May I visit you there, Anne, this summer?"

Her lips had parted as she looked earnestly at him. Jack had been reaching out to take the book from her hand so that he might draw her arm through his when Alex had appeared from nowhere. He had apparently come through the trees almost abreast of them, and had fallen into step the other side of Anne after giving his cousin a long and level look. Jack could not think of a more frustrating way to spend an afternoon than in the presence of a woman whose interest one was trying to fix while her husband looked on silently. Alex had said not a word after his initial greeting to the pair.

What Jack wanted was some outside interest. There had to be some attractive and unattached females within a radius of five miles of Portland House. It was Peregrine who thought of the vicar's brood, with whom they had all played as children. They must all be grown up by now. Surely if one rode into the village and paid a call at the vicarage, one might find two or three of them still at home. It would be a great relief to find some young people who were not constantly preoccupied with drama.

That same afternoon, then, saw Jack, Peregrine, Freddie, Prudence, and Hortense on their way to the village, the men on horseback, the girls in an open barouche. Claude had called a rehearsal for Alex and Anne alone.

Anne was the only one of the family to have memorized her part quite reliably. Even those who had only a few lines to remember had a disconcerting habit of piping up with accurate words spoken in the most inappropriate moments of the script. The duchess bullied at almost every mealtime, and Claude fumed, asking rhetorically if anyone thought he actually enjoyed his task, or if they believed that he had wanted the job in the first place, but no one ever seemed smitten enough by conscience to rush off, book in hand.

Only Freddie was apologetic. If he only had Alex's brains, he said, or even Jack's, he would be able to remember that he must not speak all his part at once, but must pause to allow other people to speak between his lines. He considered it quite provoking of Mr. Goldsmith to write a play where everyone spoke just a sentence or two and then had to pause to listen to others and remember when to start speaking again and what words to say. However, he was willing to concede that it might be all clear to him if only he had been blessed with Alex's brains.

Not only did Anne know her part, but she had thought herself into the role and thoroughly enjoyed acting out the part of Kate Hardcastle. She could not talk to Alexander in her own person. She always felt unsure of herself, unsure of his attitude toward her, and shy and tongue-tied. She felt unattractive with him, as if she were still the dull, overweight creature she had allowed herself to become when living with her brother after the death of Dennis.

Even the fact that Alexander had come to her room every night since his arrival and had made love to her each time, twice even the night before, failed to boost her confidence. Although he always stirred her to such passion and satisfied her utterly, she was not at all sure why he did so. He rarely said anything, though he always stayed for the whole night, and he was invariably grim and distant during the daytime. Did he merely wish to put the stamp of his possession on her, to remind her that she was totally subject to his will? There was never the faintest hint of love, or even of affection, in his behavior toward her.

But when she was acting, Anne could forget herself and become Kate Hardcastle, the woman she would like to be. She loved the scene in which Alexander as Charles Marlow met her for the first time, knowing that she was the daughter of the house, and was so shy that he stammered his way through the interview, not once looking her fully in the face. She loved the reversal of roles, when she could be confident and amused, helping Marlow through the interview and at the same time falling in love with his handsome person.

But today they were to practice the scene in which Marlow sees Kate dressed in her plain country clothes, mistakes her for the maid, and flirts with her to the point of an attempted seduction. She enjoyed playing along with his error, giggling and inviting his advances without in any way behaving improperly. She wondered what would happen when they reached the part in which Marlow stole a kiss from her.

But Merrick was wooden. He knew the lines for this scene. It was only halfway through the play and he had spent more time on this than on the later scenes. But he found it very difficult to throw himself into the part. Or maybe it was the other way around. He found it too easy to identify with Marlow, poor fool. Merrick had never understood how Marlow could have married Kate willlingly at the end of the play, when he had appeared an utter fool so many times in her presence. How could he have ever recovered enough self-esteem to be easy in her presence, to assert himself as her husband?

Not that he had ever before taken the play very seriously. It was an amusing piece with a very clever and intricate plot. But now, suddenly, it had taken on a very unpleasant reality for him. As if he had not appeared often enough at a disadvantage before Anne, he must now act out a part in which he became doubly foolish. He found it almost impossible to enter into the spirit of the farce.

Claude fumed and paced back and forth across the polished floor of the small ballroom in which they rehearsed. Anne was great, he said. She was Kate Hardcastle, surely as Goldsmith had imagined her. And she had never acted before, never even seen a play performed before. How could Alex be so utterly lifeless? He was flirting with a pretty woman. Then, he must flirt! It was not as if he were suddenly thrown into the company of an utter stranger. Anne was his wife, for heaven's sake. Claude's rhetoric faltered when he realized what he had just said. They all knew that Alex and his wife had been estranged from the start, and none of them knew what the state of affairs was now, though much speculation went on when the pair was not present.

"I want my tea," he blustered, covering his confusion, "but I positively refuse to allow the two of you to leave this room until you have done something to this scene. If you dare put in an appearance in the drawing room, I shall instruct Aunt Jemima to refuse to serve you so much as a cup of tea. You work it out between you. I shall return in half an hour." And he stalked from the room, leaving a startled and silent pair behind him.

The party from Portland House caused quite a stir as they rode through the village. It was generally known that the duke and duchess were gathering their family around them for a few weeks in preparation for the grand ball that was to be held in less than two weeks' time in honor of their fiftieth wedding anniversary. It was many years since all the family had been gathered together here. There had been the time when Master Alexander had lived there, a perfectly quiet and nicely behaved young gentleman until he was joined by Master Jack, Master Peregrine, and the young ladies. Then they had all been holy terrors. The only one of the whole pack who had been invariably courteous to all the lesser mortals of the village was Master Frederick, who had always stayed to smile and nod after the others had taken to their heels, having upset an applecart or done something equally mischievous. But then, everyone had suspected that poor Master Frederick did not have all his wits about him.

Now those who were on the street or close to a window as the barouche passed, followed closely by a group of horses, saw that indeed all those naughty children had grown up into remarkably handsome and fashionable ladies and gentlemen. The vicar's wife was one who saw them coming. She shrieked to her girls, who were all in the room with her, variously employed, and rushed to the study to inform her husband that the young people from the house were approaching. Her son was there too, perched on the edge of his father's desk, swinging a leg and mending a pen.

Thus it was that by the time Hortense and Patience had been helped from the barouche and the men had all dismounted and secured their horses to the picket fence that surrounded the vicarage, the buxom figure of Mrs. Fitzgerald was curtsying in the doorway, the thin, slightly stooped figure of the vicar behind her rubbing his hands together, a gaggle of girls behind them, each striving to get a view of the visitors. Only Bertrand Fitzgerald dared venture out of the house. He came bounding down the pathway, right hand extended.

"Jack, Perry, Freddie!" he exclaimed, shaking hands heartily with each one in turn. "How bang up to the minute you all look. I say, this is famous. Where's Alex?"

"Rehearsing," Freddie explained, "for Grandmamma's play, y' know. Has brains, has Alex. Big part. Must practice lots. I just have a small part. No brains, y' see. Can't hold the lines in m' head."

He spoke the last words to Mrs. Fitzgerald, who was smiling and curtsying in front of him. Bertrand had already been claimed by the girls.

"What, Fitz," Hortense cried, pushing past Peregrine, "are we invisible just because we are females? For shame."

"Well," Bertrand said, standing back and looking admiringly at his former playmates, "aren't you the grand ladies all of a sudden? I wouldn't have recognized either of you without tangled curls and smudged noses and tears in your dresses."

Jack had immediately singled out the prettiest and the youngest of the three Misses Fitzgerald. "Rose," he said, taking her hand and holding it far longer than was necessary, "the last time I saw you, you had so many freckles one might not have put a pin between them. I would not have guessed then that you would grow into such a beauty. And to think that I have already wasted three days at Portland House."

The seventeen-year-old Rose blushed deeply and smiled, totally enslaved.

"Come along, Frederick," the oldest Miss Fitzgerald said in her rather masculine, no-nonsense voice. "You shall tell us all about the play inside. Here you are blocking the pathway so that no one else can get near the door."

"How right you are, Ruby," Freddie said, looking behind him in surprise. "Damme, but I didn't notice. You're a sensible female. Always were, I remember." He allowed her to take his arm and lead him inside.

It was noticeable that all members of the party

were in a considerably more cheerful frame of mind
one hour later when they were on their way back
home. Finally they had contacted sanity and normality again.

Merrick and Anne looked into each other's eyes
for a few uncomfortable moments before he turned
away and began pacing back and forth in front of
her.

"Why must you take this whole damned thing so
seriously, Anne?" he said. "Are you trying to put us
all to shame?"

"No!" she protested. "I am merely trying to do my
best. Grandmamma wants us to perform this play
for an audience. It seems to me that we owe it to her
to make the performance as good as we are able."

"What do you owe Grandmamma?" Merrick asked,
coming to a stop before Anne and glaring at her. "A
public place in the family? Are you reveling in it,
Anne, and are you hoping that if you act like her
blue-eyed girl, she will persuade me to take you back
home with me? Is that what you want? To be the
Viscountess of Merrick, to be shown off to all the
ton?"

There were tears in Anne's eyes, but she kept her
chin up and looked steadily back at him. "No," she
said, "you know I could not be so conniving, I think.
The duchess has been kind to me, Alexander, and
she has made me feel a part of her family. I have
never before felt part of any family."

"I cannot act this scene with you, or any of the
other scenes," Merrick said. "Can you not understand that I want no part of you? How can I stand
with you here, speaking words of love and admiration, watched by Claude and frequently by several of
the others? I would prefer to be alone, trying to
forget your existence."

His words were deliberately brutal, and he turned
away as she bit her lip. He could see that she was

trying to control her facial muscles so that she would not cry before him. His words were foolish, anyway. How could he say he wanted no part of her when he could not stay away from her at night? How could he claim to be trying to forget her existence when he had made love to her each night with such obvious hunger? He ran his fingers through his hair, leaving it tousled. He took a deep breath.

"I do not know the words of the scene as well as I should," he said. "I had better sit down and read through them again before Claude returns."

"Alexander," she said. Only the slightly higher-than-usual tone of her voice indicated her distress. "Can you not forget who I am while we are acting this play? Can you not pretend that you are Charles Marlow and that I am Kate Hardcastle? Must we show everyone in your family that there is so much bad feeling between us? I shall not impose more of my company upon you than these rehearsals call for, and I shall be quite content to return to Redlands after the ball. You need not be afraid that I shall try to remain with you. Why would I want to stay where I am considered nothing? Why should I deliberately court a life of abuse and misery?"

Her face was very white and very set, Merrick noticed when he looked at her, startled. It was the first sign of spirit he had ever seen in her. He bowed formally, picked up his book from a table where he had flung it earlier, crossed to the opposite end of the ballroom, and seated himself with his back to her, the book open on his lap.

He failed to notice during the ten minutes that elapsed before the return of Claude that the book was upside down. Damn it, but he hated her. He wanted to hurt her. He had never in his life felt so out of control of his destiny. She was nothing. She was a nobody, without vitality or personality. He could no longer say she was without beauty; she was damned pretty, in fact. But she was so bland. Her answer to everything seemed to be to stare accusingly at him out of those large gray eyes, which were as often as not filled with tears. He wanted to shake her, slap her, provoke her somehow to . . . what? He did not even know. Did it matter to him what she did? He did not even want her in his life. She did not fit into any of the plans he had ever made for himself.

He was beginning to hate himself as much as he hated her. Maybe that was why he disliked her so much, in fact. He could not act like his usual self here, knowing that she was in the same house. He wanted to ignore her, or at least to treat her with the contempt that he felt she deserved. He wanted to make it obvious to her that he had wed her out of a sense of honor but that he had no intention of ever letting her share anything else of his life except his name. But she drew him like a drug. He tried to convince himself each night when he went to her that he was merely using her, displaying to her in the most insulting manner possible that to him she was a mere convenience, but the trouble was that he was too damned hard to convince.

Last night he had not even been able to content himself with having her once. He had woken up during the night to find his cheek resting against her soft curls. Her head was nestled as usual against his shoulder. He had turned his head, and immediately his nostrils had been filled with the very distinctive smell of her, that clean soap smell. He had tried to control the desire that had arisen in him as he became more aware of the warmth of her, of the softness of her flesh touching his. He had lost the battle. He had taken her almost in anger, and when she had woken with a little whimper as he thrust inside her, he had been further enflamed. He recalled now that, instead of crying with pain or fright, she had clung to him, her fingernails drawing blood from his back, her passion quickly matching his own.

She was making him her slave, and she must know it. And he hated her for it. He would not let any woman, least of all her, take away from him his freedom to control his own actions. He had ten more days of this torture to endure before he could pack her off back to Redlands, where she belonged, and begin to forget her and get his life back in order again.

Merrick turned in his chair as the door at the other end of the ballroom opened and Claude entered again. With him, surprisingly, was Grandpapa, leaning heavily on a cane and peering fiercely at Anne, who was sitting on the floor in the spot where Merrick had left her, clasping her knees and looking no older than a child.

"Now, what is this?" the duke asked gruffly. "Claude tells me that you are acting like a wooden soldier, Alex. It won't do, you know. You used to be one of the family's star turns. You two are having problems with your marriage, eh? Can't understand why, Alex. She's a pretty-enough little thing and nicely behaved."

"Grandpapa," Merrick said harshly, crossing the room again, "the condition of our marriage is a matter entirely between Anne and me. I will not permit even you to interfere in that."

"And quite right too, my boy," the duke said, looking at his grandson from beneath drawn brows, "and my marriage is my concern. At the moment the happiness of Her Grace depends a great deal on the success of this play. I don't necessarily understand why it is so important to her, but it is. And what is important to Her Grace is important to me. From now on, you will know your lines, my boy, and you will act them as What's-his-name intended them to be acted when he wrote them. And your feelings for your wife will not be allowed to intrude. Is that clear?"

Merrick's hands formed into fists at his sides as he glared back. The two men took each other's measure for long moments as the pair of spectators looked on with bated breath.

Merrick relaxed suddenly. "I always said that your bark was worse than your bite, Grandpapa," he said, "but I never knew anyone whose bark was quite so fierce. Now would you kindly leave so that Claude can start bullying Anne and me again?"

The duke left.

9 After dinner, followed by tea and conversation in the drawing room, the duchess insisted that rehearsals resume. And the following morning was no different. As soon as the stragglers could no longer pretend that they were still eating breakfast, they were informed that the small ballroom was awaiting their use. Strangely, no one grumbled on either occasion. The visit of most of the young people to the vicarage had cheered their spirits, and all were looking forward to the return visit that the three Fitzgerald girls and Bertrand had promised for the afternoon.

Even the older people were delighted. The duchess had been prevailed upon to allow them all the afternoon free. Her daughters, Maud and Sarah, with their cousin, Fanny Raine, Claude's wife, had arranged a trip into the village to see if the milliner and the haberdasher had anything worth purchasing. Claude and his brother, Martin, had agreed to play billiards with Charles Lynwood, their cousin Sarah's husband. Stanley and Celia Stewart had promised their children a walk to a hill north of the estate from which it was possible to see three different counties on a clear day.

Anne discovered the children soon after luncheon,

when she had escaped to her favorite retreat, the rose arbor. The practices were progressing much better. The outing for several of the others the day before seemed to have done them the world of good. They had somehow rehearsed their way through two whole acts the evening before, and another that morning, without too many pauses for prompting and without causing Claude a near apoplexy with their lifeless acting.

In fact, Peregrine had been downright good that morning, holding them all in stitches in the scene in which he pretended to be making love to Constance Neville for his mother, Mrs. Hardcastle's, benefit and then incurred the latter's wrath by insisting that she read aloud a letter that referred to her as "that old hag."

Aunt Maud had been good, too. One would have sworn that she was about to burst her corsets with indignation. Even Alexander seemed to have mastered his distaste of acting opposite her. When they had repeated this morning the scene that had caused so many problems the afternoon before, his manner had been almost convincingly flirtatious, and he had caught her and kissed her on the lips at the appropriate moment in the script, instead of merely grazing her cheek as he had the day before.

"Please, Kitty's ball is in the tree," a tiny voice said from beside her, and Anne looked up to see a minute girl in frilled dress and white pinafore standing before her, the large bow that held her hair at the back of her head somewhat askew.

"What's that?" Anne asked.

"Kitty's ball is in the tree," the child repeated solemnly. "Davie kicked it there after Nurse had told him to keep it on the ground. But when Kitty told him he was for it, he said a bad word. And Kitty is crying."

"Oh, dear," Anne said. "Perhaps I had better come and see if I can sort things out. Shall I?"

"Yes, please," the child said. "If Papa comes and

finds out that Davie said a bad word, he won't be allowed to come to the hill with us. And it won't be such fun to go without Davie, because I should be feeling sorry for him all the time I was there."

"I see," said Anne. "Let's hurry, then, before Papa comes, shall we?"

Kitty was indeed crying with loud wails. She was a smaller replica of her sister, even down to the crooked hair ribbon. Davie, a thin lad of about ten, stood defiantly a few feet away from her, legs apart, arms folded, looking as if he might apologize if he could only be persuaded that it was not an unmanly thing to do.

"Now, where is this ball?" Anne asked cheerfully above the wails of Kitty. "Can we reach it and get it down maybe?"

Kitty paused long enough to look up at the new arrival and point to a branch above their heads, where a bright-blue ball had been trapped by the foliage. She gave her brother an accusing glare and then began to howl again.

"Now," said Anne, "if I promise to climb up for the ball, and if Davie promises to say he is sorry for putting it there, will you stop crying, Kitty?"

Kitty stopped immediately. "He said a naughty word," she said quite steadily, and the wailing resumed.

"Well, I'm sorry anyway, you stupid girl," Davie said magnanimously. "And I can climb the stupid tree."

"No, you will not," Anne said firmly. "You have been all spruced up for an outing with your parents, I gather. The last thing you need is a hole through the knee of your stocking. And would you like to inform me what could possibly be stupid about a tree? I did not know that it had any intelligence at all that could be measured." She looked inquiringly at Davie.

"That's true, Davie," the older sister said gravely, "you must admit."

"Hush up, Meggie," the boy said, but Anne noticed that he did not include her in his opinion of the intelligence of the world around him.

Climbing a tree in a flimsy muslin dress and thin slippers was not an easy activity, Anne soon discovered. It was quite simple to climb the branches, but the twigs and leaves caught at her dress with every movement and she had to keep stopping to disentangle herself. It took fully five minutes to reach the ball and drop it down into the waiting hands of Kitty.

"Hurrah!" yelled Davie. "Is it ever so much fun up there? I am going to come back tomorrow when I don't have to be dressed in these stupid clothes."

"Oh, do be careful," Meggie urged. "You will slip and hurt yourself if you do not watch where you are going."

"Thank you for the ball," Kitty added, all traces of her tears gone. "I like you ever so much. Do you want to come to the hill with us? Papa is going to show us a view."

"I think if I can get down from here safely, I shall consider that I have done enough climbing for one day," Anne said, and began her slow and frustrating descent.

When she reached the bottom branch and had checked to see that her clothes were free from the clinging twigs before leaping for the ground below, she became aware of a pair of masculine arms reaching up for her. She looked down, startled, into the broadly grinning face of Jack.

"Romping with the kiddies, cousin?" he said. "Have I discovered your secret vice? I must say you look most charming up there. I have not seen such trim ankles in a long time. Do allow me to help you down."

"Oh," Anne said, "I had no idea of being observed. These children had a ball stuck up in the tree, you know. I was merely lending a hand. And I would really prefer it if you stood aside. I migh bowl you over if I jump when you are standing this close."

Jack continued to grin. "Do you really weigh a ton?" he asked. "I would have thought you no heavier than a feather. Come, I shall take the risk. Put your hands on my shoulders and I shall lift you to the ground."

Anne had no choice but to comply. But Jack did not play fair, she noted indignantly. He bent his elbows so that she slid the full length of his body before touching the ground, and even then she was so off balance for a few moments that she was forced to lean against him.

"I thought so," he said quietly into her ear, not bothering to explain what it was that he had thought.

Anne pushed away from him indignantly. "Thank you, Jack," she said primly.

He reached forward with both hands and carefully disentangled a leaf from her hair. His face was very close to hers. "I wish these infernal children were not so close," he said for her ears only. "I should dearly love to kiss you, Anne. You look provocatively tumbled."

"This lady climbed the tree to get Kitty's ball, Mamma," the solemn little voice of Meggie was saying.

"And Cousin Jack lifted her down from that branch," Davie added.

Anne brushed hastily at her dress to make sure that she was properly decent before looking up to smile at Celia and Stanley ... and Alexander, who was with them, his face blank.

"Really, Anne, that was most kind of you," Celia said. "But you should not have risked tearing your lovely dress. It was naughty of the children to ask, as I daresay they did. I suppose Davie put the ball up there, did he?"

"Yes, Mamma," Kitty said, "and he ... ouch!" This last as Meggie's foot caught her on the shin.

"Did he, indeed?" Stanley said dryly. "I think we

had better start this walk and work off some energy. Come along, children. Thank you, Anne."

"You have torn the hem at the back of your dress, Anne," Merrick said quietly as the family moved away. "You will want to go to your room to change. Allow me to escort you?"

Jack was left standing under the tree, a slight smile on his face.

The Fitzgeralds arrived by foot quite early in the afternoon. The girls were looking rosy-cheeked beneath their bonnets after the two-mile walk across the park. Jack immediately appropriated Rose and led her to the drawing room, where a fire had been lit against the slight spring chill. The others all followed, Hortense arm in arm with Addie, the middle Fitzgerald girl, Constance walking shyly beside them, trying to look old enough to be of their company. Jack, Peregrine, and Prudence gathered around Bertrand, while Merrick shook his hand and greeted him. The oldest Miss Fitzgerald took firm possession of Freddie's arm and marched him close in the wake of Jack and Rose.

"Come along, Frederick," she said. "Let us go indoors where at least we will be out of this wind. And do order us some tea. It is decidedly chilly outdoors."

"But you insisted on our walking here," Rose said plaintively, looking back at her sister. "Addie and I tried to persuade you that the wind would ruin our complexions."

"Nonsense!" her sister replied. "If you had only as much fresh air as you thought you needed, Rose, you would be positively puny. You and Addie both."

"I must say," Jack said, seating his companion on a love seat and placing himself beside her, "you look remarkably fine, Rose, with cheeks to match your name and eyes shining from the exercise."

"Oh," the girl said, immediately hiding those eyes beneath lowered lashes.

"I shall sit in the wing chair next to the fire,

Frederick," Miss Fitzgerald announced, ignoring his offer of a more elegant French chair close to the door. "Come and sit next to me and tell me all about London. What you have to say may not always make the most sense in the world, but I would infinitely prefer it to the silly chatter that we are likely to hear from the others."

"Well," Freddie said, "I had to have Silvester make my new yellow waistcoat. Weston refused. Said the color made him feel bilious. Said it would be no advertisement for his skills. Don't know why, though. Everybody always notices the waistcoat. So bright, y' know."

"Well," Miss Fitzgerald said, "I daresay it is not in the best of good taste, Frederick, but I am pleased that you insisted on having it made. You must always stand up for yourself, you know, even if you do not have quite as much in the upper works as most people."

"I will always do so," Freddie agreed eagerly. "Very good of you to say so, Ruby. Mama says I look like an overgrown canary in the waistcoat."

Miss Fitzgerald patted his hand. "You must wear it one day for me to see," she said, "and I shall give you my opinion. But even if I do not like it, Frederick, you must continue to wear it if you do."

Freddie gazed worshipfully at his new champion, and the conversation resumed.

"Where is Anne?" Prudence asked of no one in particular. "I wanted you to meet her, Fitz. She is very nice and very pretty, though I should not say so. She makes me feel quite the beanpole, all arms and legs. Why could I not have been petite like her?"

"Well, you are quite elegant, you know," Bertrand said diplomatically. "It's hard for a female to be elegant, Prue, when she is little."

"And she is such a good actress," Prudence continued, flashing him a smile. "You would never believe it, Fitz, but she has never even seen a play before. And she is easily our best player. She puts all the rest of us in the shade, except perhaps Perry, who is so funny. I thought my sides would burst from laughing this morning. Where is she, anyway? Do you know, Alex?"

"She tore the hem of her dress earlier while climbing a tree," Merrick said. "I escorted her to her room ten minutes or so ago to change."

"Climbing a tree!" Miss Fitzgerald exclaimed in a strident voice, pulling her attention free of Freddie.

"One of Stanley's children kicked a ball up into it," Jack explained, "and Anne was brought to the rescue." He grinned at the serious figure of Merrick, seated beside Prudence.

Anne had changed already and had sent Bella away to mend the hem of the damaged dress. She now wore a thin woollen dress of pale blue, one of her favorites. It fell straight from a high waistline and had a high round neckline. Its long sleeves were close-fitting. It was a very plain dress, and it accentuated her slimness. It was warm, at least. She had felt thoroughly chilled outside, dressed only in the flimsy muslin, without even a shawl to keep her arms warm.

She should go down. Through her open window she had heard loud voices and laughter. The visitors had obviously arrived. But she hated making a grand entrance. It had sounded as if they had all come inside. They were probably in the drawing room, and there was no way she could enter without attracting the attention of all of them. She sighed. How awful it was to have been born with such a large share of self-consciousness. It would not be so bad, perhaps, if Jack would not be there. But one could not expect Jack to miss such a large and boisterous social gathering. He was proving to be quite troublesome. Could he not see that she was not interested in his flirtation? Probably not. He was a handsome man, almost as good-looking as Alexander, in fact. She doubted that many women had rejected his advances in the past.

And if only Alexander would not be there ...
But, of course, he would be. These visitors had been
the playmates of his childhood. Anne brushed furi-
ously at the wool skirt of her dress, removing imagi-
nary pieces of lint. Nine days still to go before she
could be at peace from him again. If only she could
avoid seeing him in that time. It was a ridiculous
wish, of course. Even if she could avoid him in the
ordinary course of a day, she would have to see him
at mealtimes. And she had to look at him, talk to
him, touch him, even kiss him during the very frequent rehearsals.

And there were always the nights. She could not
avoid him then if he chose to come to her. She had
no right to lock her door against him. And he had
come each night—even last night, after their harsh
words during the afternoon. He had been very late.
She had been tossing and turning in bed for hours,
it had seemed, before he had come. He had not had
a candle with him, or lit one when he arrived. He
had not said a word, either, but had merely undressed beside the bed, undressed her, and made
love to her slowly and silently. She had reached new
heights of ecstasy with him, and he must have felt
her last cry of release coming; he had absorbed the
sound into his open mouth, which had stayed on
hers until they had both utterly relaxed. As had
become usual with her, she had burrowed her head
into the warmth of his shoulder and slept.

Many things had not changed, but Anne had. Something had happened to her as she sat on the floor of
the ballroom the day before, clasping her knees and
staring at her husband's back as he sat across the
room from her studying his part. People do not
generally change all in a rush, but something had
snapped in Anne as she sat there. Did she really love
this man who was her husband but who was in all
essential ways a stranger to her? Did he have the
right to make of her an abject, cringing creature,
who was beginning yet again to doubt her own worth?

Was she going to allow him completely to dominate her life? Was he worthy of her love?

Ten minutes can be a long time when one has nothing to do but sit and examine the state of one's life. Anne had come to the conclusion that her love for Alexander was a purely physical thing. She liked his appearance. In fact, she could not name one imperfection in either his face or physique. He was every woman's dream of a perfect man. She had no one with whom to compare him as a lover, but she was quite convinced that the world could not provide her with a man who could give her greater satisfaction. She admitted that her love for him had really dated from their wedding night and that the last few nights had been the happiest of her life. She dared not think of what the nights would be like when she returned alone to Redlands.

But having admitted as much to herself, she had tried to think of any other way in which she loved her husband. There was nothing. He had never shown her any kindness but had, in fact, often been unnecessarily cruel. He had been deliberately and brutally insulting the morning after their wedding and had left her for more than a year in a home that he obviously disliked himself. He had refused to allow her to visit Sonia or to come here for the two weeks with his grandparents. He had not spoken a kind word to her since his arrival. Yet he did not even have the integrity to leave her entirely alone, but must come to her each night, to degrade her, she supposed.

No, Alexander certainly did not deserve her love. And he did not deserve her respect. Her decision had been made during those ten minutes. He was her husband. She could not disobey him. She could not deny him whatever he demanded of her. But she was not going to allow him to destroy the very fragile sense of worth that she had built so painfully in the year and few months since he had abandoned her.

He could use her, he could insult her, but she would not allow him to break her.

In future, he would not find her so docile and so inclined to be teary-eyed before him. She would live out the nine days. She would enjoy looking at Alexander while she acted with him, and she would enjoy making love with him at night—she was not going to try to pretend to herself that she found his attentions distasteful. And when the nine days were over, she would go back to Redlands and concentrate on making the inside of the house as beautiful and as tasteful as she had made the gardens. She would make it her home and live contented with the respect of the servants and the admiration of the neighbors. She would be known as Anne Stewart of Redlands, Viscountess Merrick. And she would not in any way be in her husband's shadow. He was almost unknown there.

Anne raised her chin and looked at herself in the mirror. Yes, she decided, she even felt like a great lady already. She did not need Alexander; she did not even like him. And she certainly did not have to feel self-conscious about walking into a room where he happened to be. She swept resolutely from her bedchamber and down to the drawing room to join the guests.

"Do be a sport, Anne," Jack was saying later that evening after rehearsals were over for the day. "It is a beautiful evening, far too lovely to waste indoors. And you cannot accuse me of trying to seduce you, you know. Stanley and Celia, Freddie and Connie are coming too. But, you see, when there are three males and two females, one of those males has to walk alone. And I fear that fate will be mine if you refuse to save me from the ignominy."

Anne sighed. "You do make it sound as if it is my duty as a humane person, Jack," she said, "but I would far rather be lazy and relax in a stuffy drawing room."

"I perceive that you are weakening," he said. "Now, you cannot expect me to let the matter rest, Anne. Let me send your maid upstairs for a shawl."

"It is utter madness to go walking in the darkness," she protested.

"Nonsense," Jack replied cheerfully. "There is a near-full moon, and you must remember that four of us almost grew up here. We could find our way to the bridge blindfolded."

"Is that where you are all planning to go?" Anne asked. "The bridge across the swamp?"

"Grandmamma's claim to immortality," Jack said with a grin. "She insisted, you know, when she was a young bride that Grandpapa spend half his fortune having it built, though he protested that the bridge would be merely an expensive ornament. It really serves no useful function, you know. There is a much more convenient way around the marsh by road or footpath."

"But I agree with Grandmamma that it is a work of art," Anne said. "Very well, Jack, I shall come."

He smiled and left the room in search of Bella and her shawl. Anne was rather enjoying the situation. Alexander had sat down to play a hand of cards with the duke and Maud and Sarah a few minutes before, but he was obviously very much aware of the situation developing behind his back. He had stiffened and his head had turned to one side, as if he were listening. She was not deliberately setting out to provoke him or to make him jealous, but the new Anne was reveling in the freedom of making up her own mind about what she wished to do. She was no longer treading carefully, afraid of angering a stern husband. She had no particular wish to go walking with Jack—or with anyone else, for that matter—but she would do so just to show Alexander that she did not fear him. There was, after all, no impropriety in her acceptance. It was a family group that was going walking, and she was part of the family.

If Jack intended to monopolize Anne's attention,

he was certainly to be thwarted during the walk down the long, sloping lawns and along the bank of the stream until it widened into a marshy lake that was spanned by an elegant triple-arched stone bridge.

Freddie immediately approached her and held out his arm. "Hold on to me, Anne," he said. 'Might be some stones in the way. Wouldn't see them in the darkness. Don't be afraid of falling. I never stumble. Don't have too many brains, y' know—not like Alex— but always could see in th' dark. Cats' eyes, Mamma used to say. I don't make much conversation, mind. Not very intelligent, y' see. Nothing very important to say. But I like listening. You talk to me, and I'll try to learn. Trouble is, don't have a good memory. You'll be safe with me, though."

Jack, finding it impossible to step in between his large cousin and Anne and equally impossible to interrupt Freddie's humble monologue, helped Celia adjust her shawl and took her arm. Stanley took Constance's arm through his and patted her hand in fatherly fashion.

"What did y' think of Ruby?" Freddie asked. "Very pleasant sort of girl, I think. She don't mind that I'm stupid. She likes me."

"Oh, Freddie," Anne said, giving his arm a little squeeze, "you aren't stupid. Maybe you cannot learn or remember things as well as your cousin, but that does not make you worthless, you know. You are sweet and kind, and I believe that one might depend upon you. I am proud that you are my cousin by marriage. And you have learned the part of Diggory in the play very well."

Freddie beamed. "Damme, but you're right," he said eagerly. "Didn't make one mistake this afternoon. Jack had to be prompted three times, and Martin didn't know one scene all through."

"You see?" Anne said. "In some things you can do better than the rest of your family, Freddie."

Freddie, his self-esteem bolstered for the second time that day, picked his way along the bank of the stream with exaggerated care so that his charge would not stub her slippered toe against an unexpected stone.

"Oh, it is lovely!" Anne exclaimed as they came upon the bridge around a bend in the stream. "I have not seen it this close before."

"You have to stand exactly above the second arch to know why Grandmamma wanted the bridge built just there," Jack said, expertly maneuvering so that the six of them came up together and changed partners without anyone's seeming to realize that it had happened. Anne found herself being led onto the bridge by him. The others did not follow but continued to stroll along the footpath that would eventually circle around and take them back to the house again.

"There, you see?" Jack said triumphantly, and Anne could see in the moonlight the marsh, which looked more like a lake from this vantage point, the elm trees, and beyond them the upper lawn and the house spread out in all its majesty.

"Oh, it is perfect," she said. "How did Grandmamma know that that magnificent view of the house could be got from just this spot?" She turned inquiringly to Jack, who bent and kissed her squarely on the lips.

"I think she had it made because she thought this was a romantic spot," he said quietly. "She and Grandpapa have always been almost indecently in love, you know."

Anne moved back a step and glared. "Jack, you must stop that," she said. "I have not given you permission to take such liberties."

He leaned one elbow on the stone parapet of the bridge and smiled at her. "Can you blame me for trying, Anne?" he asked. "You are a lovely and an intriguing woman. You are such a delightful mixture of shyness and reserve on the one hand, and firmness and fire on the other. Would not a mild flirtation brighten up your time here as it would mine?"

"No," she said, "it most certainly would not."

"A pity," he said. "It's old Alex, I suppose. I never could quite see what he had that I do not, but he always had a great deal more success with the ladies than I ever had. You love him, I suppose?"

"He is my husband," she said.

He looked at her long and levelly before straightening up and offering her his arm again. "We had better catch up to the others," he said. "I would not mind the glares of Grandmamma and the glowers of Alex if I really had achieved some success with you, but it seems such a waste to be in everybody's bad books when I have merely tasted your lips and been soundly set down for doing so."

They arrived at the house arm in arm but in company with the other four. Merrick was still playing cards when they all entered the drawing room and crossed to the tea tray at which the duchess presided.

10 Freddie had been taken up one afternoon by Miss Fitzgerald in her gig. She was out taking the air and needed a companion who was more inclined to listen than to talk, she said. Jack had stolen away the same afternoon and later made a comment about Rose Fitzgerald, that could have been made only by one who had seen her the same day. Anne had been borne off to the schoolroom one morning to join in an exciting game of blindman's buff with the children. And they had all played endless games of cards and billiards, and played or listened to the pianoforte, and told and retold all of the previous week's *on-dits* from London. But on the whole, life at Portland House kept to its relentless course. Even Claude was beginning to be hopeful that they would not all make utter cakes of themselves on the night the play was to be performed.

But Merrick was thoroughly tired of the whole business of his grandparents' anniversary. Really, Grandmamma had behaved shockingly, bringing them all there under quite false pretenses. He had known that until the day before the ball, anyway, the only house guests were to be the family, and there was nothing remarkably exciting about the prospect of spending two whole weeks with one's relations. But,

really, she might have been expected to exert herself
to see that there was some entertainment for them.
There were enough families within traveling range
that visits, dinners, informal parties, might have been
arranged. And he had assumed that he would be
free to come and go as he pleased during the daytime.

Crafty old Grandmamma had got them there
merely so that she could organize theatrics and daz-
zle all her acquaintances with the talents of her family. Did she not realize that they were all grown up
now and that playacting no longer held the magic
for them that it had done when they were all children? She should have got those children of Stanley's to put on some performance. All her guests on
the night of the ball would have been suitably
impressed.

Anne seemed strangely attached to the children.
There had been that afternoon when he had found
her almost in the arms of Jack and had found out
only when he was thoroughly enraged that she had
been up in the tree rescuing a ball, of all things. And
several times since, he had seen her in the garden in
conversation with one or other of the little ones,
usually that strange, grave elder girl. When Claude
had demanded to know her whereabouts the previous morning because she was needed for a scene
that he wanted to go over, Celia had said that she
was upstairs playing with the children. Merrick had
not pictured his wife as a woman who might be fond
of children.

He was still angry with her. He had not talked to
her except when necessary or as part of the dialogue
of the play since three evenings before when she had
gone out walking during the evening with Jack. It
had been a deliberate taunt on her part, he felt sure.
She had agreed to go only because she realized he
was listening. She seemed intent on making him
jealous or angry; he was not quite sure what her
motive was. Did she really think she had the power
to make him jealous? She was his wife, that was all,

to be used for his own convenience for the few days that remained before he could send her back to the country again and return to the more congenial company of Eleanor. But he was going to make his displeasure known to her as soon as a convenient moment presented itself.

The moment came during an afternoon four days before the ball when the actors had banded together and announced that if they were to have any of their humanity remaining so that they might be gracious to the guests when they arrived, they must have some time to themselves. The Fitzgerald offspring were invited to a picnic and everyone went, except for the duke and duchess and the older generation. Even the children were allowed the treat of joining their elders. The site chosen was a large shaded lake into which the waters of the stream and the marsh finally emptied themselves. A small wooden shed, now sadly in need of a coat of paint, still held some boats, which had been much in use when the duke and duchess had been younger and when the present picnickers were children, either for circling the lake or for sailing through the navigable waterways of the marsh and under the arches of the bridge.

"Papa, Papa," Davie yelled when he discovered the contents of the shed, "take us out in the boat. Oh, famous. Can we fish?"

"You know Kitty is frightfully nervous of water," Meggie said. "It would not be fair to her if we dragged off Papa so early, Davie."

"Pooh," said her brother. "She is just a stupid girl. She can stay with Mamma and Cousin Anne. Come on, Papa."

But, as it turned out, Kitty gathered together her courage when she knew that her mamma was willing to ride in a boat and hold her close. Soon the family was being rowed from shore by Stanley, Davie loudly excited, Meggie sitting primly on her seat, instructing her brother to sit still before he overturned them all into the water.

Jack, Freddie, Miss Fitzgerald, and Rose soon followed in a second boat. Claude called after them, warning them not to go too far as it seemed likely to rain before the afternoon was out.

"I will have no use for a company of actors with hacking coughs or pneumonia on the night of the performance," he yelled.

Jack waved gaily back and put an arm around Rose's shoulder as the boat tipped alarmingly. Since the water was perfectly calm at that moment, it was not at all clear what had caused the near accident, but Jack was obviously not chancing a recurrence that might dump his companion overboard. He kept his arm where it was.

Everyone else sat down on the grass or pulled the picnic baskets from one of the gigs they had brought with them. More than one of them glanced uneasily at the sky, wondering if they would have a chance to eat before the rain came. It seemed so unfair, Hortense said, that the weather was breaking now, just when they had wangled a free afternoon for themselves. There had not been a drop of rain since they arrived more than a week before, and for most of that time they had been cooped up indoors trying to act.

"Shall we walk, Anne?" She looked up, startled, into her husband's face from her kneeling position on the ground, where she was straightening out one of the blankets they had brought with them to sit on.

"Yes, of course," she said, getting rather hesitantly to her feet and smoothing out the skirt of her pink wool dress. She picked up her shawl from the ground, where she had flung it while busy with the blankets.

She took Merrick's arm and he led her along the grassy margin of the lake, away from the marshy side. The towering old trees that grew almost to the water's edge were reflected sharply in the glassy surface of the water. There was not a breath of wind.

"It is quite lovely here," Anne said. "I do believe that if the land had been mine before the house was built, I would have chosen a site close to this lake. It seems sad that such a beautiful spot should be seen so rarely. I did not even know it existed until today."

"I am not at all pleased with your behavior, madam," Merrick said.

"What?"

"I believe you heard me," he said, "and I believe you know the causes of my displeasure."

"Indeed I do not," Anne replied, "except that you did not wish me to be here at all. What have I done, pray?"

"I am well aware," he said, "that when I met you, you were very much a spinster who had been left on the shelf, so to speak. You lured me into marriage, whether deliberately or unintentionally I neither know nor care at this late date. But I do know you are an opportunist. You saw your chance to come here and meet all the members of my family, and you maneuvered it so carefully that even I cannot accuse you absolutely of having openly disobeyed me. And I have watched you, madam, inveigle yourself into the good graces of one after another of my relatives here. What do you hope to accomplish, Anne? Do you hope that if enough of my cousins and uncles speak favorably of you to me and show disapproval of my living apart from you, I shall take you with me when we leave here?"

"Alexander," Anne said. She still held his arm, but she looked out across the lake, her chin held high. "My experience of the world has been necessarily small. I have not met a great many people in my life. But I believe I would have to travel a wide area and a long time to find another man as conceited as you. Why, pray, would I wish to live with you? So that I might gaze on your handsome person every day and tell myself what a grand catch I have made? So that I might listen to you list my shortcomings every day and grow more and more sensible of the great honor you have done me by condescending to marry me? You flatter yourself, my lord."

Merrick stopped walking and turned to face her. A quick glance showed him that they were out of sight of the group sitting on the bank. "Since when have you decided that you may talk to me like this?" he asked. "You forget yourself, I believe, madam, and to whom you speak."

"You are Alexander Stewart, Viscount Merrick, and my husband," Anne said coolly, looking directly into his eyes. "And I would you were not."

He stared at her, completely dumbfounded for a moment. "Have you taken leave of your senses?" he said. "You are my wife, Anne, whether you like it or not. If you believe you can speak to me as you wish and defy me and flirt openly with other men before my eyes, you will be forced to learn the truth in a most painful way, I can assure you."

"Flirt?" she said, eyebrows raised. "Have you really seen me flirting, Alexander? And with whom, pray? I do believe I smiled at Grandpapa this morning."

He caught her by one arm and shook her. "Come, madam," he said, "this defiance and sarcasm and assumed innocence do not suit you. My cousin Jack has been a womanizer since he was little more than a boy. He cannot resist trying to prove that he can conquer every pretty woman he meets. And it matters not to him whether the woman be married or not. In fact, I do believe he prefers his women to be already married. There is less likelihood that he will be trapped into marrying them himself. And I must say from personal experience that I can now appreciate his reasoning. Don't make the mistake, Anne, of believing that he is really interested in you. He merely wishes to amuse himself and enrage me. You make a fool of yourself by playing his game."

"Do I?" said Anne sweetly. "But then I am just the frustrated-spinster type, who has had her head turned by the practiced charms of a rake, am I not, Alexander? You should pity me, my lord, not be angry with me."

Merrick grabbed Anne's free arm and shook her until she caught at his lapels to steady herself. "Stop this!" he said through clenched teeth. "I have not seen this side of you before, Anne, and I do not like it. I will not have you behave this way before my family, do you understand?"

"Alexander," she said, still clinging to his coat, "there was a time when I was awed by your good looks and your title and obvious knowledge of the world. There was a time when I felt that if you did not love me or want me or even treat me with common courtesy, the fault must be in me. I have had much time to myself in which to think. You have kindly provided me with that time. And I have come to realize that you are a selfish and conceited man, who is not worthy of my love or even of my respect. I am your wife, as you say, and you will find that in all public ways I shall be obedient to you. I shall return to Redlands next week without a murmur of complaint. You need not fear that I shall cry and plead with you to take me to London. But in essential matters I am not part of you. I am a person in my own right, my lord, and you will not crush me again. I invite you to try."

She pulled free of his hands and moved away from the margin of the lake into the shade of the trees. Indeed, she was not as calm as she hoped she had appeared. She walked until she had reached the cover of the trees, and then she began to hurry, and soon she was running almost in panic farther and farther into the forest. He must not follow. She must not let him catch up to her and see that her control had broken. Fool! She must be the greatest fool in Christendom. All that she had said about him was true. If she had not been convinced of his overbearing arrogance before today, she had had ample proof in the last half-hour. He was insufferable. She hated him. How, then, could she love him so much? It was all physical, she told herself again and again, as if the repetition in her mind would finally convince her. If he were not so handsome, if he were not such a good lover, she would be free to hate him without reservation. She did not love him. She merely lusted after him. Her tears began to fall as she plunged deeper among the trees.

"We should get back to the others," Miss Fitzgerald said. "They will be wanting to eat tea and will be waiting for us. It would not be wise to delay. Even as it is, the rain may not hold off until we have finished our picnic."

"Oh," said Rose, pouting, "but Jack has promised to take us as far as the bridge, Ruby, so that we might walk to the center arch and see the house. I have not seen that view since I was quite a young girl."

"And now you are in your dotage," her sister said. "There will be plenty of other occasions for that walk, Rose."

"But goodness only knows when Jack will be here again," her sister argued.

"I have realized since returning here," Jack said, smiling down at Rose, "that I have much neglected my grandparents in the last few years. I am determined to mend my ways. There are many attractions to a stay in the country."

Rose blushed.

"Turn around here, Frederick," Miss Fitzgerald ordered, "and let Jack here take the oars. You are not accustomed to heavy work, and I would not wish to see you get blisters on your hands."

"Glad to row you along, Ruby," Freddie said, panting a little from his exertions. "Pleasant view from the water. I can row, y' know, as well as Jack. Can't do most things; don't have the brains. But rowing a boat is easy."

"Nevertheless, Frederick," Miss Fitzgerald said kindly, and the two men meekly exchanged the oars.

*   *   *

"Mamma," Kitty wailed, "the boat is rocking." She clung to the side with one chubby little hand and grabbed a handful of her mother's skirts with the other.

"There are waves on the lake," Davie said. "This is famous, Papa. It is like being pirates on the sea." He swayed his body from side to side, increasing the slight pitching motion of the boat.

"Sit still, my lad," his father said. "The wind is coming up and I have to row against it to get back to shore. The elements do not need your assistance."

"Kitty is frightened," Meggie explained to anyone who had not noticed. "I knew she would be. I should have stayed on the bank with her. Cousin Anne would have played with us. I like Cousin Anne."

Celia wrapped one end of her shawl around the shoulders of the tiny child who huddled at her side, and drew the rest of it more closely around herself. It was chilly out here on the lake, and the clouds were getting heavier and grayer by the minute. Stanley rowed steadily for the shore, while Davie sat in the middle of the boat, one hand on either side of it, swaying to the natural movement of the craft through the waves and trying his best to increase the size of the dips without appearing to do so.

On the bank, Addie, Hortense, and Peregrine had dragged the blankets farther back into the shade of the trees, where they would be more sheltered from the rising wind, and spread out the contents of the picnic baskets, despite the fact that neither of the two boats had yet returned and Merrick and Anne had not reappeared.

"Stanley has turned back, anyway," Prudence said, seating herself beside Addie. "There is plenty of food here for an army. I do not believe anyone will object if we have our tea."

By the time the first drops of rain began to fall,

the only missing members of the party were the two who were on foot. Everyone had eaten his fill.

"I think we should go back to the house," Jack said. "In not many more minutes this rain will be heavy and we do not have a closed carriage even for the ladies. If Alex wants to play the romantic in the woods with his wife, I say we should leave them to it."

"It is a long walk back to the house, though," Prudence said dubiously. "I believe we should wait for them."

"You all go back," Freddie said. "I shall look for them and bring them safely home."

"Rubbish, old boy," Jack said. "They are not lost, you know, and the walk back to the house will be no shorter than if you are with them."

"It was a very kind thought," Miss Fitzgerald added, "but Jack is right, Frederick. You might wander into the woods and never find them. And while you are there, getting wetter and wetter, they might well be home already steaming before a warm fire. And as Jack says, they are not lost. Alexander grew up here, after all."

"Don't like to think of Anne getting wet," Freddie said. "A delicate little thing, y' know. I like her."

"So do we all," Miss Fitzgerald said, taking his arm and leading him in the direction of the closest gig, which had already been loaded with the half-empty picnic baskets and the blankets. "But she has her husband to take care of her. She does not need you, Frederick. And we do. The rain is already coming down quite steadily. You must keep the minds of us ladies off our discomfort by conversing with us."

Jack snorted inelegantly and maneuvered Rose along to the next vehicle, an equally open gig. There was one small delay, while Freddie insisted on running back to the boathouse with the two blankets "in case Alex should think of sheltering there," as he put it. The horses were put into motion without further delay and the carriages were soon bowling along the uneven path in a race against the increasingly heavy rain and cold, blustery wind.

Merrick sat on the bank of the lake, staring out across the water until spots of rain began to land with some regularity on his hands and the back of his neck. He noticed for the first time that the water ahead of him was slate gray and choppy and that a cold wind was whipping at his hair and his neckcloth. He looked up. This was no spring shower that was approaching. There was heavy rain on the way, and from the look of the sky, he guessed that it would last all night at least. He had better go and see if he could find Anne. He did not think that she had found her way back to the rest of the party. Between him and the bend in the path that would take him in sight of the others, the trees thinned out considerably, so that he would have seen her if she had gone in that direction. She must be sulking in the woods somewhere.

He really did not want to have to face her again this afternoon. He would far rather join the others and let her find her own way back. But the rain was not going to stop. The others would be wanting to return to the house and it might take her a time to make up her mind to come back again. She might even be lost. Farther back from the lake the trees became quite dense and one could quite easily lose one's sense of direction. Not that one could be lost for long, but it could be long enough to be an annoyance to the rest of the party waiting on the bank. Merrick considered the idea of going back to tell them to leave, but he did not do so. Surely they had enough common sense not to wait. Jack, at least, thought enough of his own comfort to persuade the others to go back to the house. He took one sighing breath and headed into the woods.

Had he really treated her as badly as she had suggested through her sarcasm earlier? He knew he had. But it was so easy to excuse one's own actions, to find justification for behavior that would appall one in someone else. He had felt so bitter ever since his marriage about the way he had been forced into it and about his own weakness in not merely laughing in the face of that straitlaced brother of hers. Every day of his life since, even though he had resumed his former manner of life in London, he had been aware of the constraint on his freedom, aware that at some time he would have to do something about Anne and his marriage. And always there had been guilt about his shabby treatment of her.

Until he had been confronted so unexpectedly by her little more than a week before, he had always managed somehow to convince himself that one day he would make everything right with her. He had remembered her as a very plain, dull mouse of a woman who would probably be happy enough with her present way of life anyway. All he would have to do, he had sometimes told himself, was take her a few gifts, perhaps increase her allowance, and give her a child to fill her days with activity and at the same time to solve the problem of his own succession. As the heir to a dukedom it was his duty to perpetuate his line.

Merrick stopped and listened, but it was hopeless. All he could hear was the swishing of leaves and the gusting of the wind. He cupped his hands around his mouth and called her name several times, but there was no answer. He plodded on, looking constantly from left to right in the hope of catching sight of her. She could not possibly have returned to the others without his seeing her, could she?

His feeling of guilt had multiplied since his arrival more than a week before. She was a part of his family. There had been no reasonable argument for refusing to allow her to come. She had a right to be here, and if she was to remain his wife and was to give birth to his heir at some time in the future, it was even desirable that she meet his relatives. She would, after all, be the Duchess of Portland one day, the wife of the head of the family.

Because he had felt guilty, he had treated her unfairly. And because he now found her attractive and wanted her, he treated her in an abrupt and domineering fashion. He felt ashamed of his own desires, bewildered by his own feelings, and consequently he had turned his contempt for himself against her. But until an hour before, he had never seen himself in quite the unfavorable light she had described. Was he arrogant? Selfish, yes. He would admit he had been that. But arrogant? Did he think himself vastly superior to her? Would he have treated her the way he had if he had not considered her unworthy of him?

Where was she? The canopy of leaves over his head no longer protected Merrick from the rain, which was now sheeting down and dripping from his hair down his neck. He wore no hat. He did not know whether to plunge on into the wood, which became thicker and more tangled with undergrowth ahead of him, or whether to walk parallel to the lake in the hope that she had stayed in the area of more open trees. He gambled on the belief that she would have chosen the latter course, and walked on after calling her name yet again in vain.

She had claimed that she would not wish to live with him even if he would allow it. She could never love or respect a man such as he, she had said. The idea was totally new to him and uncomfortably humbling. He had always thought that his chief cruelty to her had been keeping her away from his presence. And now that he put the thought into words in his mind, it did seem quite insufferably arrogant. Did he think he was the answer to any maiden's prayer? Why would she want to live with him? Had he ever spoken a word of kindness to her since the day he had proposed to her and lied about his true motives for making her an offer? Think as he could, he could not remember one word.

She liked his lovemaking, though, did she not? There could be no mistaking the eagerness of her response each night over the past week and more. He had never, in fact, known a woman who so openly enjoyed a sexual encounter. But did that alter any of the facts? He enjoyed her too, but that fact had made no difference to his resentment of her and his desire to hurt her. Perhaps they were just two people who were unusually compatible sexually but who had no other point of contact.

Merrick almost missed her. She was standing quietly against a tree trunk, her hands clasping her shawl across her breasts, her hair plastered to her forehead and neck. She was looking silently at him. He would have walked on by if her dress had not been pink and a noticeable contrast to the colors around her.

"Did you not hear me call?" he asked. "Why did you not answer?"

"Yes, I heard you," she said, "but I did not wish for your company."

Merrick strode toward her, his face setting into hard lines. "What did you plan to do?" he asked. "Stand here and commune with nature all night?"

"I will shelter here until the rain passes and then walk home," she said calmly.

"You are soaked," he said, "and this rain is like to last all night and all tomorrow too. There is no point in standing here. Come, let's go."

Anne bit her lip. He was obviously right. She had been telling herself for all of five minutes that she should move, but she had heard him calling and she did not want to be seen. But now it seemed childish to argue, to explain to him that she wished to be left to find her own way home. She stepped away from the tree, tried to pull her shawl even more closely around her, and began to walk in the direction from which he had come.

Merrick shrugged out of his jacket. He wore only silk shirt beneath it. "Here," he said, "take off your shawl. It is saturated, I see, and will bring you no warmth. My coat is still dry on the inside. Put it on."

"Don't be foolish," Anne said, hurrying on and refusing to relinquish her hold on her shawl. "There is no reason why you should make yourself uncomfortable for me. Put your coat back on."

Merrick grabbed her by the arm and pulled her to a halt. "By God, Anne," he said, "I do not know what has got into you today, but I have no patience left. Take your shawl off immediately and put on my coat. I will take no more of your nonsense."

"I am sorry," she said, removing her shawl. "I did not know you were giving an order, my lord." She took his coat and put it around her shoulders, but she did not put her arms inside the sleeves. She walked on.

Merrick ground his teeth. It was just as if he acted a part when he was with her. She made him into a tyrant. He had meant for once in their relationship to do her a kindness. He followed her and placed an arm firmly around her shoulders so that he could guide her along the shortest route back to the picnic site. She did not try to disengage herself from his touch.

The place was deserted, of course. Merrick had not expected that anyone would have waited for them. But there was a two-mile walk back to the house and they were already shivering from the cold and wet. They would go into the boathouse for a while. It was unlikely that they would find there anything more than a temporary respite from the wind and rain, and there was no way he could build a fire, but even the thought of temporary shelter was welcome at the moment. His shirt was clinging to his body like a second, unwelcome skin, and he could see Anne's hair dripping down into her face and down her neck inside the collar of his coat.

Anne made no objection to being taken to the boathouse. She felt more miserably uncomfortable than she could ever remember feeling, and believed that she would rather lie down in the soaking grass and wait for death than plod on to the house, which must be miles away. For a few moments the inside of the shed felt like the interior of heaven. There was no wind and there was no rain. It felt almost warm.

"Ah," Merrick said through chattering jaws, "someone was thinking. They left us the blankets." He bent down and scooped up a blanket that Anne could hardly even see in the darkness of the shed, and tossed it to her. "Take off your dress," he said, "and wrap yourself in this. Wring out your shawl and take the worst of the drips from your hair with it."

Anne was too thankful for the promise of dryness and warmth to argue. She turned her back on him and peeled off her clothes before wrapping herself completely in the blanket. But she still had to clamp her teeth together to prevent them from audibly clacking together.

"Come here," Merrick said.

She could see him in the semidarkness, standing against the overturned hull of one of the boats. He too had a blanket draped around him.

"Why?" she asked.

"You feel warm at the moment only because of the contrast with what you were just feeling," he said. "It is really miserably cold in here, and the thickness of one blanket is not going to do much to hide the fact. We will have to share body heat for a while."

"No," she said. "We must start back soon if we are to be home before it is dark."

"Anne," he said, "I do not intend to do any more walking in the rain for a while. If someone had sense enough to leave these blankets for us, I am sure the same person will eventually send a carriage for us, especially if we are not back by dinnertime. I intend to make us as comfortable as possible until it arrives. Come here."

Anne came and was immediately enfolded, blanket and all, within his covering. He pulled her down to the floor, where they sat, their backs propped against the side of the boat. He was right, she found. Her nose and her wet hair soon registered the fact that it was cold inside the hut. She allowed her head to burrow its way into the blanketed hollow between his neck and shoulder. They sat silently for a while.

"Will Grandmamma not worry?" she asked at last.

"Worry?" he said. "Why would she? You are with me, are you not, and I am your husband. The worst she will imagine is that we will catch cold and not be able to speak our lines in four days' time."

"Should we not start walking, Alexander?" she suggested. "I feel warm now. I am sure it would be better to leave and get back to the house, where we can find dry clothes."

"I feel warm too," he said, "and comfortable. I say we stay."

There was silence again, during which time Merrick turned a little toward her and pulled her further into the warmth of his body. "We seem to make a habit of getting caught in storms together, Anne, do we not?" he said, brushing his nose against her damp hair.

She did not answer but could not for the life of her have stopped lifting her face to him after a while, knowing even as she did so, just as if she had lived it all before, what would happen when she did so. They looked deeply into each other's eyes, questioningly, and then their lips met in a light, searching exploration. He was so warm. His breath was warm on her cheek, his lips against hers, his tongue circling her own and stroking against the roof of her mouth.

She moved back from him to allow his seeking hand to open the blanket that was wrapped around her and roam over her shoulders and down to her breasts. She could feel her nipple harden against his palm, and her own hands spread over the muscles of his chest and shoulders. This was ridiculous. It was one thing for him to come to her at night, a man claiming his conjugal rights. It was quite another for them to be kissing and fondling like this in broad daylight on the dirty floor of an old boathouse. She pushed at his chest.

"What is it?" he said, his eyes heavy as they looked into hers. "Are you not comfortable?"

"Don't, Alexander," she said. "Someone may come."

He laughed. "It would be an everlasting shame, would it not," he said, "for someone to find me in close embrace with my wife? But don't be afraid; we will hear the approach of horses for quite a distance. I shall have you chastely wrapped in your blanket again by the time anyone comes here."

He continued to smile at her, and Anne was mesmerized by the charm of such an expression directed fully at her. Her resultant hesitation was her downfall. Before she had a chance to argue further, his mouth was teasing hers again and his warm hand had strayed to her other breast to work its magic there. When he pushed impatiently at her blanket and brought her against his naked chest, she did not protest.

When the ache of their desire could no longer be satisfied with mouths and hands, Merrick slipped to the ground, taking the hard coldness of the floor against his back, and lifted Anne astride him so that he might cushion her body against his own warmth. But he was unaware of either the discomfort or the cold as he plunged them both into the world that they could find only together. He paced himself almost by instinct to the tensions of her body, allowing himself release only when he felt hers coming, seeking her mouth with his at the moment when he knew she would cry out.

Afterward, when he held her still-trembling form wrapped in his arms, cradled on his body, Merrick still felt no discomfort. He lay staring at the rough boards that made the roof, one of them rotted in a corner so that the rain dripped through to form a small puddle, as he felt Anne relax fully and her breathing become even. Anne. Was he going to be able to leave her in five days' time? He had not wanted her, had fought all these days against his growing need of her. But he feared that he was losing the battle. It would be hard to go back to Eleanor, who would, as always, chatter gaily to him while undressing and resume the conversation almost without break a minute after he had finished having intercourse with her. There was something very flattering, and utterly satisfying, about holding in one's arms a woman who slept as a result of one's lovemaking.

He raised one arm behind his head and with the other hand absently massaged her head through the damp hair. He could take her back with him just for the Season. If he tired of her within those few months, he could then send her back to Redlands. It would give him some pleasure to introduce her to the activities of town, to clothe her in the height of fashion. He would even derive some pride out of introducing her to the *ton* as his wife. Perhaps he would. He had a few days in which to think about it. It would certainly make amends in a small way for his treatment of her thus far. Life must be insufferably dull and lonely at Redlands.

Although his arm was cramped and the rough surface of the floor had made its presence felt through the blanket that lay between it and him, Merrick was almost sorry to hear the sound of approaching horses. He would have liked to watch Anne wake up and to have had the leisure in which to kiss her. She felt deliciously soft and warm. He shook her slightly.

"Wake up, sleepyhead," he said, "or someone is going to discover to his embarrassment that we really are man and wife." He rolled sideways and set her down in a sitting position on the floor. He laughed as she pushed his hands away and drew her blanket tightly around her.

Both of them were on their feet when Freddie pushed the door open. "Damme," he said. "Knev you would be here. Told Grandmamma so. 'Alex has brains,' I said. 'He will take Anne to shelter in the boathouse.' I was right."

"Grandmamma is here?" said Merrick, peering through the crack between the opened door and the side of the hut. "Then I had better put my shirt on or she will have an apoplexy. Good lad, Freddie, you brought a closed carriage. No, you don't," he said, turning to Anne. "I shall carry you out just the way you are. And you may take that as a command, madam."

11 Two days before the play was to be performed, Lady Sarah Lynwood decided it was high time to perform the duties that her mother had assigned her almost two weeks before. She did not have an acting part, as she was much given to fits of the vapors when excited. Instead, she had been put in charge of the costumes. Actually, it was not a difficult task. The duchess was a hoarder; nothing was ever thrown away at Portland House if there were any possible use left for it. Even clothes that no longer fit or that had fallen out of fashion were packed away carefully in trunks and stored in the attic rooms if they were not suitable for giving to the servants or to the poor.

Thus Sarah had a wide choice of gorgeous garments in the styles of several decades before: skirted and satin coats, knee breeches, buckled shoes, and wigs for the men; wide, panniered skirts, tall wigs, feathered plumes, and even some patches for the ladies. All she needed to do was match up sizes and choose suitable styles and colors for each character.

Anne was the only other adult who seemed at all interested in helping. She was intrigued by the old-fashioned finery, which she had seen only in pictures before. Had people really worn all these heavy and costly clothes not so long ago? Somehow, when she really thought about it, she could almost imagine Alexander's grandparents as young people, dressed for a ball. They must have been a stately pair. Even now they both moved around with something of a regal bearing, as if they had learned from long habit as young people that they must keep their shoulders back and chins up if their wigs were to stay in place.

Anne went up to the attic with Sarah during the afternoon. The three children were with her. Meggie had found her in the rose arbor during the morning and told her very solemnly that Aunt Sarah would not allow them to look at all the old clothes upstairs, though Mamma had said that she was to go up later in the day to open up all the trunks. Kitty was crying and Davie was calling her a stupid girl and had called Aunt Sarah a bad word, though no one had heard except his sisters. Anne had winked at the child and promised to see what she could do. The children had been granted permission to come, provided they did not interfere with the serious business of their aunt.

Sarah picked out a kingfisher-blue satin gown for Anne to wear as Kate Hardcastle, grand lady. Through most of the play she would wear a plain outfit, borrowed from the housekeeper and taken in quite ruthlessly at the seams. But for one scene in the play, the one in which Alexander as Charles Marlow would know who she was and stammer his way through an interview with her, she must look as regal as possible. The skirt was very wide, a large bow gathering the fabric into a bustle at the back. The bodice looked as if it must be almost indecently low.

"Ah," Sarah said triumphantly, bent low over another trunk, "here are some hair plumes, Anne. They must have been made to match that gown." She drew out plumes of blue and green.

Anne laughed. "How ridiculously long they are," she said. "I should have to stoop to go through doorways with those in my hair."

"Especially when you are wearing that wig," Davie said, pointing to the piled creation that lay in a heap next to the gown.

"Do try them on," Kitty pleaded. "Please, Cousin Anne. We may not even see you all dressed up on the night. When we asked Mamma if we might watch the play, she said only that she will see."

"Yes, do let us see you," Meggie agreed.

Anne giggled. "I shall certainly not try on the gown up here," she said. "I shall need a great deal of help getting into that. But I will try the wig and the plumes. I shall feel so ridiculous."

Sarah was far too busy rummaging through the numerous trunks for likely costumes for the other characters to take any real notice of what went on behind her. It was left to the children to help Anne fit the wig; there was no mirror in the attic. Finally it was adjusted to the satisfaction of Meggie, the most critical member of her audience. Anne then sat down on the floor while the children placed the plumes in her hair.

"No, no," Sarah said during one moment when she had withdrawn her attention from a trunk, "plumes are meant to stand straight up, dears, to give a lady height, not float out behind like a tail. Worn like that, they would hit everyone in the eye who came within ten feet of her."

"Pull them out carefully, Davie," Meggie instructed, "or you will disturb the hair. Stay still, Cousin Anne. You are very patient. You are almost ready now."

"Oh," Anne said, turning her head as soon as the children had withdrawn their arms, "the box of patches. I should be quite undressed without a patch, you know. Come, you shall help me choose one."

Even Meggie was giggling when they finally settled on a black patch in the shape of a heart and placed it carefully close to the corner of Anne's mouth. Anne stood up and curtsied deeply to the children, being very careful to keep her head rigidly upright.

Davie clicked his heels to attention and made her

an elegant bow. "May I have this dance, madam?" he asked, while Kitty clapped her hands and jumped up and down and Meggie watched, her head on one side.

"Damme," Freddie's voice said from the doorway, "you look as fine as five-pence, Anne. Don't she, Alex?"

Merrick was standing, one shoulder leaning against the doorframe, his arms folded across his chest. "Rather top-heavy, I would say," he said, his eyes sweeping her from head to toe, and Anne became self-consciously aware of how ridiculous she must look with such elaborate headgear and a simple cotton day dress.

"Came to see what you have found for me, Mamma," Freddie said. "Is there a waistcoat the color of Anne's gown? It would look grand. Will I wear a wig too? How famous." He crossed to his mother's side and peered into the trunk in which she was currently rummaging.

"Cousin Anne is wearing a patch," Kitty said, raising wide eyes to Merrick. "We helped her choose it. It is a heart."

"Is it, indeed?" Merrick said, strolling into the crowded room and looking closely at the patch. "So it is. Ladies used to wear patches, you know, to pass along a message. The color, the shape, and the place where she put in on her face were all chosen for a purpose."

"Really?" Davie said, gazing with interest at Anne's face. "What message is Cousin Anne sending, do you think?"

"A heart is for love," Meggie said.

"Precisely," Merrick agreed, "and I think the placement close to the mouth is an invitation to be kissed. Would you not agree, Davie, my boy?"

"But what would black signify?" the boy asked as Merrick's eyes met and held Anne's.

"Black is for evil," Meggie said.

"Black is for mystery," said Kitty.

"Black is noticeable," said Merrick. "Perhaps the lady merely wishes to make sure that the invitation will not be missed."

"But it was a jointly made choice," Anne protested. "And we really had no choice of color. All the patches in the box are black."

"I think you should kiss Cousin Anne," Davie said, grinning, to Merrick.

"Yes, kiss her, Cousin Alex," Kitty agreed eagerly, clapping her hands.

"Adults don't kiss. Only children," Meggie added.

"Well," Merrick said, "sometimes all of us can be children. If Anne can be enough of a child to dress up and play at being at a ball with Davie here, she can also be child enough to be kissed." He leaned down and placed his lips against hers for a slow moment. There was a gleam of something that might have been amusement in his eyes when he straightened up, though he did not smile.

The children shrieked their amusement.

"Now it is time for me to join in the games," he said. "I came here with Freddie to find out what horrors Aunt Sarah is resurrecting for me. Ah, a tricorne. Is that for me, Aunt? I think I rather fancy that. Tricornes worn with wigs were so much more dashing than top hats, don't you agree, girls? Let me show you."

Anne dislodged the plumes from her wig and removed the headpiece and the patch unnoticed while the children and the two men turned their attention to the small pile of garments and accessories that Sarah had lifted out onto the floor.

Miraculously, no one had taken cold during the afternoon of the picnic, though all of them had, to a greater or lesser extent, had a soaking. Most of them had soon warmed up before the drawing-room fire and with the aid of brandy for the men and steaming tea for the ladies. Anne had been the only one over whom the duchess had really fussed. In fact, when she knew that Anne had been left behind with her grandson at the site of the picnic while the others came home out of the rain, she had roundly scolded them all and insisted on accompanying Freddie in a closed carriage when an hour had passed and it had become obvious that the pair must either have met with some accident or have taken shelter somewhere.

The duchess had been horrified when she saw her grandson emerge from the boathouse carrying his wife bundled up in a blanket. She had not even commented upon his shocking dishabille, but had lifted Anne's feet to the seat of the carriage, so that they would not receive any of the draft from the doors and had chafed her hands all the way home. Despite Anne's protests, she had insisted that Merrick carry her up to her room, and soon a whole string of maids were carrying hot pitchers of water to the room for a bath and hot bricks to warm the bed, where Anne was banished for the rest of the day. As a result of the treatment, or in spite of it, she had not suffered any ill effects from her exposure to the rain and cold.

No physical ill effects, that was. But during her enforced stay in her room, she had nursed other wounds. It was so easy to tell oneself that one would be sensible. It was so easy to say that her love for Alexander was only physical and that it therefore was of no real importance. It was easy to tell herself that after five more days she would be glad to go home so that she might be free from her imprisonment to her own desires. It was another thing entirely to convince her emotions to agree with her reason.

She loved Alexander. Despite what he was and what he had done to her, despite everything, she loved him, and the thought of being separated from him again soon, perhaps forever, was one she did not dare let her mind dwell upon. She was becoming so dependent on his presence. The mere sound of his voice or the simple knowledge that he was in the same room could brighten her day and torture her all at the same moment. Although she was trying to avoid him except when contact was absolutely necessary, she knew that really she was not trying as hard as she might. She was much more successful at avoiding Jack, probably because she really wished to do so.

Life was going to be unutterably dreary when she went home alone. There would be no chance contacts, no possibility that perhaps sometimes he would look upon her a little more kindly than was usual, no chance that occasionally they might share a smile. And the nights were going to seem endlessly empty without Alexander to love her, without the warmth and comfort of his body against which to curl into sleep.

She wished the afternoon had not happened. It had seemed much more intimate to be with him in the boathouse during the daytime than to have him in her bed at night. It had seemed far less as if he was merely using her as any man might use his wife. She could almost have imagined as he had kissed and caressed her before entering her that he had done so out of love. And he had smiled at her when she had tried to withdraw from the embrace, instead of becoming angry as she had half-expected. She was no longer able to tell herself that he had never shown her any kindness. She had not missed his motive in taking her on top of his body for their coupling. He had taken the hard floor against his own back. She ached for him, for his love, for some sign that she was more to him than a mere convenience. She very much wished that the afternoon had turned out differently.

No, she did not, of course. Her life was going to be a lonely and a barren business. And her memories of these two weeks at Portland House would be painful ones. But would she exchange this life, unsatisfactory as it was, for the life she would have had if Alexander had not been stranded at Bruce's home? It was very unlikely that she would ever have married, and her life at this very moment would be intolerable if she had not. Bruce had recently wed the daughter of the vicar in the village where he taught. Anne would have been in the unenviable position of being a spinster in the home of married relatives.

She was far better off as she was. Redlands was her home and she was undeniably mistress there, loved as well as respected, she had reason to believe. And she had a husband who was able and willing to pay all her bills, with the result that she could make of the old, shabby building a home that pleased her love of beauty. And she had her memories: memories of her wedding night, when she had given herself up to ecstasy, believing herself loved; memories of a family that, for all its oddities, was close and filled with affection, and that had extended that fondness to her; and memories of two weeks in which she had known physical fulfillment with her husband and in which she had seen him in a somewhat more sympathetic light than she had ever before seen him. Memories were a poor substitute for present happiness, but they were at least something.

It was, then, with a determined cheerfulness that Anne had joined in the almost feverish preparations of the final few days before the grand ball. She patiently went over and over a scene when Claude was dissatisfied, when tempers were generally running short. She helped the duchess sort through the cards that had been returned in reply to the invitations that had been sent out, though she did not know quite to what purpose they did so. She played with the children and took them for a long walk in the lime grove, when everyone else either ignored their existence or snapped at them for being underfoot. She gave her attention to Freddie when he was fretting over the decision of whether to wear his puce satin waistcoat beneath his gold evening coat at the ball, or his pink-and-blue-striped one. And she desperately clung to every contact with her husband, committing every word, look, and gesture to memory for future reference.

It was a result of her kindness in giving Freddie some attention that Anne became his confidante. He had brought his evening coat and the two waistcoats to the library, where she sat alone, by prearrangement. It was the morning after the search of the attic for their play costumes.

"Oh, I think definitely the puce, Freddie," Anne said, having given due consideration to both garments under consideration. "It is so much more distinguished than the striped for an evening function. And it complements the gold of your coat so much better. What do you think?"

"Grandmamma will frown and say something cutting if I do the wrong thing," he said. "But if you say so, Anne, the puce must be the better. You would tell me the truth. You have taste. Always look lovely. Lucky man, Alex. Brains, you know. If I had brains, perhaps I would have married you, Anne."

"Brains have nothing to do with the matter, Freddie," Anne said kindly. "Any woman would be fortunate to be your wife. You have the gift for making someone feel special, and you do not need intelligence for that."

"Do you think so?" Freddie asked eagerly. "Damme, I thought no woman would ever have me. Do you think Miss Fitzgerald would consent, Anne?"

"Miss Fitzgerald?" Anne repeated, taken aback. "Are you thinking of asking her, Freddie? Indeed, I am sure she is very eligible."

"And pretty," Freddie said. "Do you think she is pretty, Anne?"

Anne considered. "Well," she said carefully. "No I would not say she is pretty, Freddie. Handsome, I think, would be a more appropriate description."

"Yes," he said. "By Jove, yes, she is remarkabl

handsome, is she not? Do you think she will have me, Anne?"

"I cannot answer for her," Anne replied, "but I would think her very poor-spirited if she did not, Freddie. Unless." She paused to make sure that he was giving her his full attention. "Unless she does not love you, you see. Sometimes it is possible to like someone terribly, but not to love him. And some people do not wish to marry those they do not love. Do you understand me, Freddie?"

Freddie's brow creased with concentration. "What if someone loves someone else, but does not like him?" he asked. "Do they marry?"

"Oh, yes," she said gently. "Quite frequently, I am afraid."

He looked at her. "Like you and Alex," he said, arrested by the thought. "That's it, isn't it, Anne? If you were mine, I would like you and love you, y' know."

"Thank you, Freddie," she said, for some absurd reason fighting tears. "And can you do the same for Miss Fitzgerald?"

"Oh, yes," he said, his eagerness returning. "She is a remarkable female, Anne. She will look after me. But she don't bully me. Told me I should wear my canary waistcoat even if no one else likes it, provided I like it myself."

"Did she?" said Anne. "She is a wise lady, Freddie. When do you plan to make your offer?"

On the day of the ball life became fevered. Claude positively insisted that all the actors attend a final rehearsal of the play after luncheon in the small ballroom. It was fortunate for him that he had made this wish in the form of a definite order three days before, because there were many other activities that might have distracted his actors. All of them had their preparations for the ball to attend to. And there were many visitors arriving. Most of the guests were coming from distances close enough that they could arrive merely for the evening functions. But many were coming from London and needed to stay overnight.

The lure of meeting these old acquaintances was strong upon the actors, but Claude was adamant, and the duchess declared that she did not wish to see one of the pack of them until at least teatime. The duke too cleared his throat loudly at the luncheon table and said that since this was the duchess's wedding anniversary, everything must be as she wished. As if matters were not always that way, Jack muttered to Peregrine.

The rehearsal was a disaster. Freddie kept forgetting to pause between his speeches to allow others to play their parts; Martin as Mr. Hardcastle, the bore, overdid his part to such an extent that Jack declared the audience would all drown him out with their snores; Maud as Mrs. Hardcastle played her indignation with Peregrine as Tony so well that her waving fist actually did connect with his nose and drew blood; Prudence as Constance Neville became so furious with her play lover, Jack, that she stamped her foot and called him "horrid man" just at the moment when she was supposed to be weeping sentimental tears over being parted from him for three whole years; Jack made fun of everyone and everything and continually leered and waggled his eyebrows at Prudence; Peregrine played the clown and threw himself down on the stage, clutching his sides and laughing insanely every time the script called for some merriment; Merrick was wooden again and bumped Anne's chin painfully when he was supposed to bow formally over her hand; and Anne, according to Claude, appeared dull and frightened instead of pert and bouncy in her interviews with Merrick as Charles Marlow.

Claude was complaining of an upset stomach and a splitting headache by the time they had limped and clowned their way to the end of the play. He declared that they would have to cancel the whole proceeding and let the duchess fume and scream. It was Freddie who saved the day.

"The same thing used to happen at school," he said. "I used to sing in the choir." Jack snorted, but Freddie continued, apparently not having noticed. "The last practices were always terrible. Sopranos squeaky. Altos off key. Choirmaster never worried. 'Boys,' he used to say, 'if your last practice is poor, I know you will be good on the day. If your last practice is good, I start to worry.'" Freddie beamed and Jack applauded.

"'Out of the mouth of babes,'" he said. "Bravo, Freddie, my lad."

Merrick sighed and sat down heavily on a chair. "Go and drink several cups of tea, Uncle Claude, and get yourself ready for dinner. We will all be too nervous tonight to do anything wrong. We would be too terrified of Grandmamma's wrath, anyway, if we dared do anything as reprehensible as forget a line. Not to mention Grandpapa. I have the feeling that tonight he might really prove to be the ogre that Grandmamma always makes him out to be if we do anything to spoil her day."

"And we promise for your sake to do our best," Anne said, smiling at Claude. "You really have worked very hard, Uncle Claude, and have been very patient with us. I may speak only for myself, but I must say that these two weeks have been very happy ones, working with almost the whole family on a project like this. I thought it would be quite impossible when Grandmamma first mentioned it."

"Do let us go to the drawing room for tea," Hortense pleaded. "We are missing all the new arrivals and the latest news from town."

Anne would have retired to her room, suddenly shy at the knowledge that the house was full of strangers. But Merrick crossed the room to where she was quietly piling the books, which were no longer needed, and extended his arm to her without a word.

He had made a decision, and he was intending to put it into effect immediately.

In the drawing room the duke and duchess were holding court with obvious relish. They were surrounded by friends of other days, some of whom they had not seen for several years. The room became suddenly much overcrowded and loud with greetings when it filled with the family members who had been acting their play.

Merrick placed Anne's hand on his sleeve and circled the whole room, speaking to each new arrival in turn. All appeared to know him so well and so freely called him Alex that Anne shrank closer to his side, wishing that she could disappear in the process. But he would not allow her to remain either invisible or anonymous. He constantly drew her forward and introduced her as his wife. She was smiled upon and spoken to until her mind was bewildered and she gripped Alexander's arm as if it were a lifeline.

The duchess's eyes were frequently on the pair, and she smiled rather smugly as she conversed with those closest to her chair.

12 Forty people sat down to a very early dinner that evening, the performance of *She Stoops To Conquer* having been set for eight o'clock. The male actors left the dining room with the ladies, so that they might be ready in their costumes by the time the dinner guests had drunk their tea and port, and the outside guests had arrived. Claude had to ask his actors what the main course at dinner had been; he could not for the life of him remember. No one answered him.

Hortense was the first to be ready in her maid's outfit. She went to help Anne dress in the elaborate lady's outfit that she was to wear for the first part of the play until she changed into the housemaid's dress that her father in the play preferred. Bella had been loaned to some of the guests from town who had come without their own maids, though she would be in Anne's room after the play to help her dress for the ball.

"I am more than ever glad that Grandmamma saw fit to give me a small part," Hortense said. "Are you not positively petrified, Anne? Has your mind not gone totally blank?"

"Don't," Anne said. "I refuse to believe that I have forgotten my part, and I have no intention now of trying to recall lines, just in case I might find that you are right. Do help me with these buttons, Hortense. There must be at least two dozen of them down the back."

The peacock-blue gown was soon in place, the panniers evenly arranged over her hips and the bow neatly centered at the back. Anne tugged ineffectually at the bodice to try to cover her breasts more completely.

"Do you think I should wear some insert here?" she asked Hortense, gazing anxiously into a mirror.

"Definitely not," the girl replied. "You look quite ravishing, Anne. All the men will be ogling you."

"Oh, dear," said Anne.

The wig came next. Hortense helped her adjust it snugly over her own curls and then carefully powdered it before inserting the plumes so that they stood proudly above her head. Anne hesitated over the patch box. Was it really necessary to wear a patch? It would be hardly visible to the audience, anyway. However, she finally found herself placing the heart shape beside her mouth again and turned away from the mirror before she should lose her spirit and peel it away. She caught up the peacock-feather fan that the duchess had brought to her the day before after finding out that Anne was to wear her old blue gown, and was ready to go. Her stomach felt rather as if the arms of a windmill had got inside it and were turning. She still dared not try to remember any of her lines.

All the actors were assembled behind the stage that had been set up at one end of the small ballroom, except Freddie. Peregrine announced that he was still undecided about which waistcoat he should wear. Sarah had found him a white one to wear beneath the plain black coat that he must have as the servant Diggory, but Freddie felt that his costume was too plain. He had been wearing the canary one when Peregrine had gone to accompany him downstairs, but even Freddie had realized that that partic-

ular waistcoat was unsuited to a servant. He had
been considering a lime-green one when his cousin
had lost patience and come downstairs without him.

"Alex," Claude said with ominous calm, "go upstairs and find that nincompoop without delay. Tell
him that I want him here inside the white waistcoat
within two minutes, or within five minutes he will be
wearing-it inside his throat."

Merrick grinned and left.

The ballroom was filling up with chattering, gorgeously clad ladies and gentlemen. Anne sat bolt upright on a chair. She dared not lean back for fear of
crushing her bustle, and she dared not move her head
lest plumes or wig or both come tumbling down about
her face. She would be able to relax more, she felt,
once her first two scenes were over and she could
change into the plainer but by far more comfortable
housemaid's dress. She looked about her. Everyone
did indeed look quite splendid clothed in the fashion
of half a century before. There seemed to be something so much more stately about those earlier styles.

Alexander had left the room, having gone in search
of poor Freddie. But Anne had noticed every detail
of his appearance in the few minutes during which
they had been in the room together. She had always
considered that his thick dark hair contributed largely
to his handsome appearance. But tonight she found
his powdered wig, tied at the neck with a black
ribbon, quite suffocatingly charming, especially when
he had carelessly put the black tricorne on his head
while helping Martin rearrange his neckcloth. His
long brocaded waistcoat beneath a well-fitting skirted
frock coat also suited his tall, well-built figure to
perfection. Had she not loved him before, she would
surely have fallen in love with him tonight, she
thought with disgust.

"Aunt Jemima and Uncle Roderick have just made a
grand entrance," Claude announced, blanching noticeably. "We should be ready to begin in five minutes'
time."

And they all became aware of the hush that had begun to descend beyond the curtains that divided the stage from the rest of the small ballroom. Merrick reentered the room with Freddie in tow almost at the same moment. Freddie was wearing a white waistcoat.

"Oh, you do look distinguished, Freddie," Anne said.

Freddie beamed and both Merrick and Jack grinned. Martin and Maud stepped onto the stage and took up their positions for the opening scene.

Freddie had been quite right. The performance proceeded quite flawlessly if one ignored the fact that Freddie, Hortense, and Constance, who were supposed to be caught in a fit of the giggles when Mr. Hardcastle mentioned one of his old jokes, really did become hysterical and laughed for much longer than the script called for. Freddie said afterward with some indignation that he could have remained perfectly serious if the audience had not laughed so loudly and destroyed his control.

The members of the audience had come out for an unusually festive evening. Many of them had attended a lavish dinner earlier and all of them would be attending a large and elaborate ball later. It was a special treat, even for those who had come from the busy social life of town, to be entertained with a full-length and well-known drama between the two events. No one had come prepared to be overly critical. The humor was laughed at, the romance smiled at. The fact that the hero and heroine were a husband and wife who had never been seen together before ensured that extra attention was paid to the main romantic scenes, and several people actually applauded when Merrick caught his wife around the waist and planted a kiss on her lips when the character he played mistook her character for a maid in the Hardcastle house.

But it was Peregrine who stole the show. Everyone

took one curtain call at the end. Merrick and Anne
and Maud took two, and Peregrine three. The audience had roared with laughter at his treatment of
the scene in which Tony Lumpkin takes his mother
by night in a wide circle around the house while she
believes that she is thirty miles from home on
Crackskull Common surrounded by highwaymen. At
his third curtain call, Peregrine sang again a raucous and rather vulgar song that he had sung at the
Three Jolly Pigeons inn during the play.

It made a fitting ending to what had really been a
very jolly middle part of the evening. Claude declared after the curtain had been closed for the final
time and the stage was suddenly strewn with wigs
and fans and buckled shoes that had proved too
tight for the wearers, that the duchess had actually
had tears in her eyes at the end of it all and that
even the duke had looked suspiciously bright-eyed.

"And so they should," Jack said. "Shedding a few
tears is the least the old tyrants can do after ruining
a perfectly decent couple of weeks for us all. The
next time I am invited down here for an anniversary
I shall remember a quite pressing previous engagement."

"Oh, nonsense, Jack," Hortense said. "You know
you have loved every minute of it. And tonight you
were positively basking in the glory of being so much
in the limelight. You know very well that all the
ladies will be falling over themselves to dance with
you later on, now that they have seen how dashing
you looked on the stage."

"Sisters!" Jack said, his eyes turned skyward.

The duke and duchess came through the doorway, the former supporting himself very heavily on
an ivory-handled cane. "You were all quite wonderful!" the duchess said. "In fact, I do not know quite
how we got out of the habit of gathering here every
Christmas and having theatrics. We really must start
again."

"Grandmamma," Jack said, "I have no wish to be

rude, but if you wish us to be present to see you and Grandpapa open the ball, you must allow us to go upstairs to dress."

"Are you really going to dance with Great-aunt Jemima?" Prudence asked the duke, saucer-eyed.

"You think I am incapable of doing so?" the duke barked, glaring at his grand-niece.

She laughed and hugged him as she followed her cousins and other relatives from the room.

Merrick was in the main ballroom long before most of the other actors and actresses put in an appearance. He was dressed in a black, closely fitting evening coat and knee breeches, looking quite conspicuous among the brightly colored clothes of most of the other men present. Only the vivid whiteness of his lace cuffs, silk stockings, starched shirt points, and elaborately tied neckcloth relieved the severity of his outfit. But there was nothing dull about his appearance, if the many glances he was receiving from a large number of ladies were any indication.

The duke and duchess were still in the receiving line. The dancing had not yet begun, though the hour was well advanced. Merrick spoke to a large number of acquaintances, but he waited impatiently for the arrival of his wife. He had thought of going to her room so that he might accompany her downstairs, but he found himself unaccountably shy of doing so. They did not yet have a normal husband-and-wife relationship, despite the fact that they had shared a bed for the past two weeks. He could not bring himself to walk into her dressing room, where her maid would probably be fussing over her. So he had come down alone to await her in the ballroom.

He felt restless and strangely excited. He wanted her with him as he talked to acquaintances. He wanted people to see them together; he wanted everyone to know that he claimed her as his wife. He had found more and more in the last few days that his eye followed her whenever she was in his view and tha he had a greater awareness of her presence in a room than of anyone else's. When he had become conscious of the fact, he had asked himself why it was, and the answer had fascinated him. He found her beautiful, desirable, charming.

He was proud of her, proud that she belonged to him. He had noticed with the pride of possession that the other members of his family liked and even admired her. And he had seen the reason why. Anne was a kind and warmhearted person, a fact that was not immediately evident because she was quiet and unassuming. But Freddie responded to her, and the children were constantly hanging about her skirts when they were not confined to the schoolroom. Jack treated her with noticeably more respect and less flirtatiousness than he had at first. And the rest of the family appeared to accept her and love her as if she had always been one of their number.

Merrick had decided two days before that he would keep his wife with him and make a proper marriage of their relationship. He had not yet told her. He planned to do so this evening. It would be a fitting occasion on which to pledge themselves to a new life together. She was planning to return to Redlands the next day and talked of it quite freely to other family members. He had kept to himself the knowledge that he would be able to hand her a last-minute reprieve. She did not know that she would be spending the rest of the spring in London, tasting all the delights that the Season had to offer. She did not know that he planned to lavish his money on her, buying her clothes and jewels and anything else that her heart desired. Perhaps when the Season was over he would travel with her and show her places and treasures that she had only dreamed of seeing.

He could hardly wait. Merrick smiled and bowed toward a couple of dowagers, who had found themselves comfortable chairs against the wall and were obviously settled for a comfortable coze, probably at the expense of many of the guests present. He had

been looking forward to this part of the evening
even before the discovery he had made earlier in the
evening. He supposed it was Freddie who had caused
it all. Anne's comment on his white waistcoat when
he had entered the room had been so obviously
calculated to make the poor man feel good about his
costume that Merrick had had to smile. But looking
at Anne, sitting in such a stately fashion on the edge
of her chair, her back ramrod-straight, her wig and
plumes looking so delightfully elegant, the black patch
close to her mouth so provocative, he had been surprised by a totally unexpected rush of tenderness.
How utterly sweet she was. And how he loved her!

The feeling of wonder had stayed with him throughout the play. As he acted out his part, he had fallen
in love with Anne as surely as Charles Marlow had
fallen in love with Kate Hardcastle. Of course he
wanted her with him after this night was over. And
of course he would want her after the Season was
over. He would want her for the rest of his life. And
so he waited for her arrival in the ballroom with
impatience, longing to see her, to touch her, dance
with her, talk to her, and eventually to tell her the
truth. Finally he would be able to treat her without
the cruelty that had plagued his relationship with
her. He had it in his power to make her happy, to
make amends for the past. Through his own fault,
she had lived a dreary and a lonely life for more
than a year. He would see to it that she had everything that money could buy and love offer for the
rest of her life.

Anne, meanwhile, was ready and excited. She had
been to some parties and balls on a small scale as a
young girl. But she had never prepared for anything
on such a lavish scale as this. She had been busy and
preoccupied with the play all day, but even so, she
had been aware of the fevered activities going on in
the house in preparation for the ball that evening.
She had been passing through the downstairs hall at
the same moment in the day as a seemingly endless

string of footmen were carrying huge armfuls of flowers in the direction of the ballroom, and she had peeped into the room on her way upstairs after tea to find that it was transformed into a magnificent garden that quite took her breath away.

Until the play was over, she had not had much time to think about the ball itself, but now she found herself somewhat nervous. It was several years since she had danced, and she had really not had much practice at any but country dances. She had never danced or even seen the waltz, which she heard was now all the rage. She hoped that she would not make a cake of herself by tripping all over her own or her partners' feet—if she had any partners, that was. She hoped that at least a few of the gentlemen would ask her to dance. Freddie surely would, and Stanley and probably Claude and Jack.

It seemed likely that Alexander would dance with her once, for form's sake. She hoped so. She was going to need all the memories she could collect after tomorrow. All that was left was this evening and the night. And the night would be short, with the ball beginning so late. It would be dawn, probably, before they went to bed. Their final night of love. Perhaps there would never be another. Anne gulped down a feeling of panic and won for herself a tut of disapproval from Bella, who was trying to clasp together a stubborn string of pearls around her neck.

Perhaps the whole evening would be a disaster, Anne thought. Perhaps Alexander would take no notice of her at all. She recalled the moment of alarm she had felt during the afternoon when he had been introducing her to a bewildering array of strangers. She had been feeling shy but happy to be on his arm, being presented to people who knew him well. But as soon as he had introduced her to Lady Lorraine Walsh and her new husband, she had been jolted. The very lovely, poised young lady before her was the girl to whom Alexander had been

betrothed when he married her. Sonia had told her
that. And she was in the house at this very moment
and would be present at the ball. Perhaps Alexander
would be paying her lavish attention. Perhaps she
would see beyond any doubt that he still loved the
girl. How would she be able to live with that knowledge afterward? The recollection of that would blot
out all the other lovely memories with which she was
to brighten the days and years ahead.

The reflected image of Bella was staring at her,
eyebrows raised. Anne got to her feet and crossed to
a long mirror, in which she could see the full effect
of her gown. Yes, Bella had been right, as she usually was. The sea-green lace overdress over the royal-
blue silk gown looked quite stunning. The lace had
been caught up with small bows at intervals around
the hem, to show the rich color of the underdress.
She wore very little else to ornament her person.
Blue slippers, a blue ribbon threaded through her
hair, her pearls, and long white gloves completed the
outfit. Anne stared at herself with satisfaction. She
still had not got over the novelty of being slim. The
high-waisted style of the dress, with its short, puffed
sleeves and low neckline, made her feel positively
dainty.

Anne slipped past the receiving line and entered
the ballroom feeling nervous and conspicuous. Familiar faces from across the room immediately beamed
at her, and an elegant exquisite, dressed all in gold,
bowed in front of her and complimented her on her
acting ability. And then Alexander was at her side
and she smiled up at him with the sheer relief of no
longer feeling completely isolated. He was smiling
back, and her heart did a somersault.

"I hope you have reserved the first set for me," he
said, taking her hand and laying it on his sleeve.
"How beautiful you look, Anne. You quite put into
the shade all these ladies in their insipid pastel shades."

She hardly had time to look up at him in surprise
before the orchestra could be heard tuning up in the

minstrel gallery and the duke and duchess appeared in the ballroom.

"Is Grandpapa really going to dance?" Anne asked. "Surely he will never be able to do so."

"Grandpapa has a will far stronger than any bodily ailment," Merrick said dryly. "I'll wager that he will dance the whole set before collapsing for the rest of the night. You and I will be expected to dance in their set, too, my dear. I am Grandpapa's heir, you know."

"Oh, no," Anne said, shrinking back. "I am not a dancer, Alexander. I shall not be able to remember the steps, especially if I know that we are the focus of everyone's attention. It would be far better if you led out Aunt Maud or Aunt Sarah or one of your cousins."

"Nonsense!" Merrick replied. "I will be expected to dance the opening set with my wife. And Grandmamma has instructed the orchestra to choose a tune that is not excessively lively so that Grandpapa will not find it too great a strain. It will be slow enough to give you time to remember the steps. Keep your eyes on Grandmamma and follow what she does. I shall help you, too."

Anne followed him apprehensively to the center of the floor, aware of eyes directed at them and aware that her husband had claimed this first dance only because it was what was expected of him.

13 Two hours after the start of the ball Anne was feeling flushed and happy. She had not dreamed that she would be in such demand as a partner. She had not sat down since entering the room, and she had not danced with the same partner twice. Alexander, before leaving her at the end of the first set, had written his name in her card for both the dance before supper and the one after. And her card had quickly filled completely. She had been complimented on her appearance, on her acting, and even on her dancing by one young man whose own dancing skills suggested that he was hardly an expert critic.

She was standing now with her arms on the stone balustrade of the terrace outside the ballroom, enjoying the cool air on her cheeks and arms. Freddie stood beside her, leaning against the barrier, looking back toward the ballroom.

"So it is all settled," he was saying. "I am the happiest man alive, Anne. She knows I don't have brains, but she'll have me anyway."

"Indeed, I am very happy for you," Anne said. "Miss Fitzgerald is a very sensible lady, and my opinion of her good sense has increased in the last minute. Any lady would be fortunate to have won your love, Freddie, and she must realize it."

Freddie giggled. "She told me at first that she can bring no dowry and I must consider very carefully," Freddie said. "As if that would make any difference to me. Can you imagine, Anne? Dear Ruby!"

"Are you to make the announcement tonight?" Anne asked.

"Can't," Freddie replied. "Wouldn't be able to get the words out in public, y' know. M' mind would go blank. Can't ever remember things. Don't have too many brains, y' know. Not like Alex. And couldn't get Ruby to make the announcement. Wouldn't be fitting."

"No, it would not be fitting," Anne said.

"Besides," Freddie said, brightening, "haven't talked to the reverend yet. Her father, y' know. Must talk to her father tomorrow. Ask for her hand. The proper thing to do."

"Yes, you are quite right, Freddie," Anne said. "I had not thought of that. How clever of you."

"Ruby says we will get married during the summer," Freddie said. "Splendid idea. Addie and Rose will be able to come to London for next Season. We can find them husbands. Or Ruby can. Not me. I ain't got the brains to do it, but Ruby will know who is suitable for them. Splendid girls, Addie and Rose." He beamed.

"What a very kind thought!" Anne said. "You will be a quite wonderful brother-in-law, Freddie. Those girls are very fortunate."

"Have to go dance with Grandmamma," he said as the music from within the ballroom drew to a close. "Grandpapa is in the card room. He was roaring for someone to bring him a cushion to put under his leg when I saw him. Grand person, Grandpapa. Brains, y' know."

Before Freddie could escort Anne back inside the ballroom, they were joined on the terrace by Jack.

"Ah, here you are," he said to her. "The next set is

mine, I believe. You may run along, Freddie. Grand-mamma is loudly predicting that you will probably have forgotten that you are her next partner and that she will end up being a wallflower. Go and convince her that she is as much in demand as she ever was as a girl."

When Freddie had left, Jack turned to Anne and grinned. "Did I arrive just in time to save you from death by boredom with that intellectual giant?" he asked.

"I perceive that you enjoy having a joke at the expense of Freddie," Anne said, "but I shall not allow it. It seems to me that all his life people have been telling him that he is some kind of half-wit, and he was come fully to believe it. He may not have a great deal of intelligence, but he has something infinitely more valuable. He was sweetness and kindness and humility and I would choose him before an intellectual or a wit any day."

Jack's grin did not falter. "Anne," he said, "you are quite adorable when you are angry, you know. I apologize most humbly. I should have known you would take that idiot's part. I have noticed how you will go out of your way to try to make him feel good about himself. Why will you not do the same for me?"

"I think you already feel quite good enough about yourself not to need my assistance," she said.

"I have not felt particularly good about most of this fortnight," he said. "I have finally met a girl for whom I could feel a serious affection, and it turns out that she is already married to my arch-rival and cousin."

"Nonsense, Jack," Anne said. "You do not at all fit the image of a tragic lover. You wished to flirt with me and had your nose pushed a little out of joint when I showed you that I would have none of it. I suspect that rejection does not often come your way. You are too handsome and too charming for your own good, you know. And at this moment the goose bumps on my arms are so large that I fear they may burst at any moment. Please take me inside to dance."

Jack sighed. "I could suggest a much more pleasurable way to warm you up, Anne," he said, "but I know when I am beaten. I did not realize at the start that you care a great deal for Alex, but you do, and I suppose he has a right to you. But I do think it a crying shame. Why could I not have been caught in that snowstorm?" He offered his arm and led her into the stuffy warmth of the ballroom.

The next dance was the supper dance. Anne found her spirits lifting as soon as Jack left her in search of his next partner. She would be with Alexander now for the whole of one set, for all of supper and again for a set. She must make it memorable. She must notice the touch of his body, the expressions on his face, the words he spoke. This would be almost her last contact with him. After this, there would be only his presence in her bed for the little that would remain of the night by the time the dancing was over and all the guests had left. One more chance to be with him and one more chance to make love with him. Then perhaps endless years at Redlands.

It was a waltz. Anne had danced one earlier with Stanley, who had shown great patience when he had realized that she was unfamiliar with the dance. For the first part of the set he had danced only the basic steps with her, until she had caught the rhythm of the music and felt more confident. Only then had he taken her through some wild turns and twirls. Now she felt confident that she would not make a fool of herself.

It was really quite blissful. They did not speak at all, but there was no awkwardness in the silence. Alexander held her very firmly and led her through the waltz so confidently that she felt she would have floated along with him quite faultlessly even without the earlier lesson with Stanley. She became less and less aware of the other people in the room and of her surroundings in general, and more and more aware of the man who held her, the man who had become everything in life to her. She had tried not to let it happen, had tried to convince herself that her need for him was merely physical and that his character was not one that could arouse true love in her. But unfortunately, she had found, one's heart will not always listen to one's head, and the heart is inevitably the stronger of the two.

She was in love with Alexander, hopelessly and utterly in love with him, and she was no longer going to try to deny it. She would have this hour and this night, openly and vulnerably in love with him. The hurt of being alone again from tomorrow on was not going to be any the less if she refused to admit the truth to herself. She might as well open herself fully to the pain.

There was a general movement toward the supper room as soon as the waltz was finished.

"Are you hungry?" Merrick asked.

Anne shook her head.

"Let us walk in the garden, then," he said. "May I fetch you a shawl?"

"I shall get it," said Anne, and ran lightly up to her room. How well this hour was turning out for her. Instead of having to share her husband with a roomful of other people during supper, she would have him all to herself. Not that he was likely to talk any more than he had during the dance, but at least they could walk together. She would be able to feel his presence, store away one more memory.

They did indeed walk in silence for a while, crossing the lawn at the side of the house until they came to the cobbled walk before the house and then angling off toward the rose arbor. Anne snuggled inside the warm wool shawl that she had fetched from her room, though one of her arms was drawn snugly beneath his and held to his side. She wished that they might never speak, that nothing might ever happen to break the spell, the illusion that they were a normal married couple, in harmony with each other.

"Bella has your boxes packed?" Merrick asked at last.

"Yes," she said. "It was lucky that this shawl was close to the top of one of them. I will not keep the coachman waiting tomorrow."

"Perhaps we will give the coachman an extra day off," he said.

Anne looked up at him, a query in her eyes. "You think I shall be too tired to travel," she said. "I think not. Grandpapa's carriage is so well-sprung that I shall probably sleep on the road. Anyway, I shall be able to sleep all I want when I get home to Redlands."

"And if I tell you that you will not be going to Redlands?"

"What do you mean?" Anne asked.

"You are not going back there," Merrick said. "You will be returning to London with me the day after tomorrow."

Anne stopped walking to turn and stare at him. "Why?" she asked.

"Why?" he said with a laugh. "I tell you you are going to London rather than to Redlands and you ask me why? Because I have decided that it shall be so. That is why."

Anne searched his eyes, a pain in her throat that made drawing breath almost a physical effort. "No," she said. "Please do not do this to me, Alexander."

The remains of his smile disappeared instantly.

"Always," Anne said, having difficulty with her breathing, "always you must play the tyrant with me. You have always hated me, have you not? Even when you married me. You treated me with quite calculated cruelty the day after our wedding and then you abandoned me for more than a year. I believe you would have been well contented never to see me again, Alexander. But I have been forced on your attention once more. And now you find that you have not yet wreaked enough revenge on me for taking you away from your chosen bride. I did not miss noticing tonight that you have danced with her

twice already. And so you must take me to London
with you. Why, pray? So that you can flaunt your
flirts and your mistresses before me? So that you can
continue to humiliate me by showing me constantly
that you have only one use for me?"

Merrick stood very still looking back at her, his
face shuttered. "It appears to me," he said finally,
"that you have not objected overmuch to the use to
which I have been putting you. Or has your acting
ability this fortnight extended beyond the stage and
into our bed?"

Anne could feel herself flushing and was thankful
for the darkness that surrounded them. "No," she
said, "there has been no acting involved. You are a
very good lover, my lord. I would guess that I am
receiving the benefit of the lessons you have learned
from a countless number of light-skirts. This has
been a very pleasurable two weeks, but I fear that
tedium would set in if the period were extended.
You see, Alexander, I have used you in the same
way as you have used me." Anne smiled and turned
to enter the arbor.

Merrick was after her in a moment, grabbing her
arm and turning her roughly to face him. "It is not
true," he said. "You merely speak this way because I
have hurt you and you wish to salvage your pride.
Admit it, Anne. I can force you to do so, you know."

She laughed in his face. "Poor Alexander," she
said. "It is quite beyond your understanding, is it
not, that any female could resist your charms. Have
you ever crooked a beckoning finger before and
been rejected? You are much like your cousin, Jack,
you know. Earlier this evening he, too, was forced to
admit that he had failed to add me to a string of
conquests. It is ironic, is it not, Alexander? Poor
ugly, mousy, fat Anne Parrish! Take me to London
if you wish. I shall enjoy the experience enormously.
But every time you come to my bed, my lord, know
that I am merely using you for my pleasure. In my

heart I shall hate you as I have since the morning after my wedding."

Merrick's grip on her arm relaxed. "I had thought to show you some kindness," he said. "Perhaps the best kindness I can show you is to send you back to Redlands?"

"Yes," she said, and her shoulders sagged suddenly. She could feel the fight draining out of her. "Let me go back home, Alexander. It is too late for kindness. Let us only not hate each other. If you force me to live with you, I shall truly grow to hate you, I fear."

He stared at her for so long that she was afraid she would lose control and hurl herself at him. But finally he nodded. "I see," he said. "I am sorry, Anne. I did not fully understand until now. You shall go home tomorrow. I shall not burden you with my presence again."

Silence stretched between them again, a silence during which they continued to stare at each other. And all the unexpressed feelings and the unspoken words were locked inside him and he had no way, no right to speak them. He had forfeited the right more than a year before when he had bedded her and so callously insulted her and left her the morning after. He had forfeited the right every day since, every day during which he had done nothing to show a husband's care for his wife. He had hoped that tonight he would be able to start making amends, but he had not had the chance to say any of the things he had planned. He had been stopped very effectively by her anger and bitterness, her utter rejection of him. And he could not fight back. He had no right. The only way he could show his love now was to leave her, to allow her freedom from his presence.

Anne. He stared at her, at his wife, whom he loved, whom he had thought to have with him for the rest of his life. But this was it, the end. Instead of a lifetime with her, he had only a few more seconds. Very soon he must turn and walk away, and he must never force his presence on her again. He might never see her again. He could never tell her how much he had grown to love her, how much he wished to spend the rest of his life making up to her part of what he had taken away from her since he had stumbled in on her during that winter storm.

"Good-bye, Anne," he said, holding out his hand to her, willing her to accept the handshake. Their final touch.

She looked steadily back at him. "Good-bye, Alexander," she said, and she inhaled with deliberate slowness as she placed her hand in his. Probably the last time she would ever touch him. She held the inhaled breath and let it out with steady control as he raised her hand to his lips. A moment later, it seemed, he was gone, without another word and without a backward glance.

The whole of the star-studded sky above Anne's head and the branches of the trees that ringed her wheeled with dizzying speed around her and she sank to her knees onto the gravel of the arbor path. Her face and hands were wet with her hot tears even before the first sob tore at her throat and chest.

Anne did not return to either the supper room or the ballroom. She did not even consider the discourtesy she was showing to the gentlemen who had signed her dance card for the sets after supper. She went straight to her room, rang for Bella to tell her that she would not be needed again that night, undressed, and climbed into the four-poster bed. She lay diagonally across it for the remainder of the night, facedown, knowing that he would not come, yet taut with expectation through the long and sleepless hours after the music ceased and the sound of voices and laughter died away. She did not sleep at all.

She was the first of the family to leave. The duke's best traveling carriage drew up outside the house just before noon, and everyone gathered either in the hall or on the cobbles outside to kiss her and wish her a safe journey. Even some of the guests who had stayed overnight after the ball were there. But Merrick was not.

Anne saw it all through a fog of exhaustion and distress. She hardly knew that she smiled as she kissed and hugged everyone and had a personal word for each. She hardly realized that she gave an especially big hug to the children and to Freddie, whose eyes were bright with unshed tears. She did not notice that the duchess was unusually tight-lipped and quiet or that the duke, leaning on his cane, looked more thunderous than usual. She knew only that the coach was the haven that she must reach, that once she was inside with the curtains drawn and once it was in motion, she would be safe again and could let go this tension that threatened to tear her apart.

She hardly realized, as she stood on the steps of the carriage, that she looked back at the people gathered in the courtyard and at the empty doorway and at all the windows along the front of the house. She did not look out again once she was inside. She did not wave to anyone.

PART THREE

December 1816–February
1817

14 Viscount Merrick huddled inside his many-caped greatcoat, trying to keep his neck warm. His beaver hat was drawn over his brow. The snow, fortunately, was not as bad as it had been in that storm a little more than two years before when he had first met Anne. Too wet to settle on the ground, it melted on impact. But it felt deuced uncomfortable against his cheeks and eyes, and was inclined to melt slowly down the back of his neck as soon as it came in contact with the warmth of his body. And it impeded visibility, so that his eyes were narrowed against the falling flakes, almost unable to see the road ahead.

As on the previous occasion, he had had ample warning that the snow was on the way. Heavy snow clouds had lain over the city all of the previous day and had been even heavier and more gray that morning. He should not be on the road at all, he knew. He was fortunate that conditions were not a great deal worse than they were. But the truth was that it was the weather that was directly responsible for his being where he was at the moment. For a month he had been making up his mind to travel to Redlands. Christmas would perhaps be a good-enough excuse. But he had let Christmas pass. How could he burden

187

her with his company for such a festival? Then he
had thought that perhaps the beginning of a new
year would be an appropriate time to pay a visit. But
that occasion probably would have passed too if the
apparent imminence of snow had not finally decided
him the day before. It was the last week of December
already. There was a distinct possibility that if snow
fell, it would last for a long time and halt all travel
between London and Redlands. Then, not only would
he be unable to reach her in time, but no messenger
would be able to reach him. Although there were all
of ten days left, such events were unpredictable, he
had heard. It was bad enough to think of not being
with Anne for the birth of their child. It was quite
intolerable to know that the child might be born and
he have no way of knowing the fact perhaps for days
afterward.

So he had decided to come. She probably would
not welcome his arrival. It might agitate her to know
that he was in the house when she delivered the
child. He certainly had little right to be there with
her. He had treated her abominably during both of
their encounters and had forced her into a pregnancy that was doubtless unwanted. But he could
stay away no longer. He had ached to be with her
from the moment he had opened the letter in which
she had informed him that she was with child. He
had worried constantly about the state of her health,
had written to her several times to ask her how she
did. But she had always answered briefly and courte-
ously, had always told him that she was well.

Finally he had resorted to writing to the village
doctor who attended her—she had refused his offer
to bring her to London so that she might be attended by a London physician. But the doctor, too,
had merely assured him that his wife was in good
health and was like to deliver a healthy infant at the
end of her time.

Merrick had wanted almost desperately to be with
her during the months of her pregnancy. Life had

not been pleasurable for him since those weeks during the spring at Portland House. He had taken up his old life in London, attending as many parties, sporting events, and meetings as he normally would. But their power to bring him contentment had disappeared. He had ended his liaison with Eleanor within a few days of his return to town and had felt no great urge to begin a new one or even to indulge in casual beddings. There was only one woman he wanted, and she was beyond his reach. He could have forced himself upon her. He knew, in fact, that she was not totally averse to his person. He had the legal right to be with her. But he could not believe that he had the moral right. She did not like him and had demonstrated quite clearly that she wished to live apart from him. He punished himself by honoring her wishes.

But he had to break his own self-imposed exile on this one occasion. He must be present when his child was born. He owed the infant that. And he was terrified for Anne's safety. Death in childbed was distressingly common, even with ladies of the upper class. How would he ever be able to live with himself if that should be Anne's fate? How he expected to stop such a disaster by his mere presence at Redlands he did not know, but he felt his nearness to her to be essential.

Even through the snow, Merrick could see that landmarks were becoming more familiar. For the remaining few miles of his journey he hardly noticed the discomforts of the elements. His mind was totally absorbed with the scene that faced him. How would she react when he arrived in the middle of the evening like this, quite unannounced? Would she be angry, upset, cold? Even faintly glad to see him? How would he explain himself? He hoped that he would be able to establish a friendly relationship with her, at all events. He was very much afraid that n the embarrassment he would feel, his manner night be aloof or imperious. He had never been able to feel at ease with Anne. And how could he be so now? He had not seen her since that scene in the garden of his grandparents' home on the night of their ball. She would be very large with his child now.

Merrick did not let go of the heavy knocker outside the oak doors of his home until he heard someone at the other side pulling back the bolts.

"Never was I more glad to see the inside of a door," he said, pushing his way past an astonished butler into the light and comparative warmth of the spacious hallway.

"My lord," Dodd said. "We little expected to see you on a night like this. Why, you might have been lost in the snow."

Merrick was peeling the gloves from his hands and tossed them and his beaver onto an oaken chest that was close by. "Where is her ladyship?" he asked, pulling impatiently at the buttons of his damp greatcoat. "Is she in the drawing room?"

The butler gaped. "You did not know, my lord?" he said. "But of course you could not. Her ladyship, my lord, is, ah . . ." He stopped to cough delicately. "Her pains are upon her, my lord. She is in her chamber. The doctor is with her, and Mrs. Rush."

Merrick blanched and tossed his greatcoat toward the chest, not seeing the outstretched arm of Dodd. "My God," he said, and the butler turned to watch him take the stairs to the daytime apartments and then those leading to the private apartments three at a time.

Anne had been amazed at first to discover that she was with child. Yet it had not taken her long to be equally amazed that she had never considered the possibility. During those two weeks when Alexander had been at Portland House, they had made love each night except the last, several times more than once. It had not taken her much longer to be thrilled by the knowledge. She had been wretchedly unhappy in the weeks following her return home, desperately trying not to contemplate the long and lonely years ahead.

It had not helped to know that she had had the chance of a different life. She could have gone to London with Alexander. There were times when she almost wished that she had agree to go; surely an unsatisfactory marriage was better than no marriage at all. But during all her more rational moments she knew that it was better to be away from him than to be with him, knowing herself despised and probably disliked, capable of satisfying him in only one way. Had she not loved him so much, perhaps she could have borne it. She believed that she was not very different from many other wives. But she did love him and consequently she exiled herself from him.

Yet now she would have part of him. The warmth of their intimacies would live with her for nine months, and afterward she would have his child to suckle and hold. She would have another person on whom to lavish all her love, and that person would be part of the man she loved most in all the world. She hoped that the child would be a boy. Alexander would at least respect her if she could produce an heir for him. More important, perhaps a boy would look like him, and she could delight in seeing the father in the child. A few times the possibility entered her head that Alexander might take the child away from her if it were male, but she ruthlessly suppressed the thought. He could not be so cruel.

The months had been solitary ones for Anne. She had only the household staff for company most of the time. She had accepted a few invitations from neighbors until she felt her condition was becoming obvious, but afterward she had hardly gone beyond the confines of her husband's estate except to attend church on Sundays.

The months had been solitary but not lonely ones. The ache of longing for Alexander that had driven her almost insane for several weeks had gradually dulled in the face of the symptoms of her condition: the unusual tiredness, the slight nausea, and finally—and gloriously—the first movements of the child within her womb. Her life had become more placidly contented than she could ever remember it being. She had spent countless hours dreaming of what it would be like to have a baby in the house, a child to bring noise and disorder and laughter into the ordered quiet of her life.

Anne had not immediately written to inform her husband of her condition. She had not known quite how to broach the subject and had not known how he might react. It was only when she received an invitation to the wedding of Freddie and Miss Fitzgerald that was to take place in September that she realized that the truth must be told. She had wished to attend because she had grown very fond of Freddie during the two weeks of their acquaintance and because she had come to love the whole family. But she could not go. Alexander would be there, and she could not risk meeting him again. Her resolve might crumble. She would have to use her pregnancy as an excuse, to stay away. So finally she had written to Alexander two days before penning a refusal to attend the wedding.

She had been surprised at his reaction. His reply must have been written the same day as he received her letter. It had been impossible to detect his feelings from the words he had written, but he had made lengthy and detailed inquiries into the state of her health, and he had seemed to realize the reason for her decision not to travel to Portland House for the wedding. He had urged her to go if she felt well enough to make the journey and had offered to stay away himself if she felt that his presence would be distressing to her. Anne had stayed firm on her decision, but she had been strangely touched by the offer. She did not normally associate sensitivity with Alexander.

It had not been merely her pregnancy and he

dreams that made the months tolerable for Anne. She had not been idle during this time. The grounds outside the house had been made attractive, so that anyone approaching the house along the long and winding drive was given the impression that the owners lavished love and attention on their property. Now she had turned her attention to the interior of the house, determined to make it a place of taste and elegance as well as a bright and comfortable home.

Heavy and faded draperies had been pulled down from windows, and old and threadbare carpets rolled up from the floors. New items had been ordered to replace them. Paintings and family portraits that had been crowded into an upper room that boasted neither size nor light had been moved to the upper gallery, where they immediately took on a new glory. Priceless seventeenth-century tapestries that had been removed from the dining room a few generations before in the belief they were old-fashioned had been replaced and immediately gave a new luster to the family silver and crystal. The Wedgwood china collection that had been partly hidden for years in a heavy wooden cabinet had been displayed openly around the living apartments. And old furniture that seemed to add only gloom to the rooms had been reupholstered and transformed. The list of improvements went on and on.

By the time Anne was heavy with child, her love for Redlands had converted into a great pride. She could wander from room to room and stroll around the grounds, muffled up warmly against advancing winter, and feel that it was her home and surely the equal of almost any of the grand estates in England. It was a place fit for the son of a viscount, grandson of a duke. It was a place in which she could contemplate with peace of mind spending the rest of her days.

Her time came upon her quite unexpectedly, ten days before she had expected to begin her labor. It was a gloomy morning when she came down to an early breakfast after a night in which she had slept little. It was so difficult to find a comfortable position in which to sleep, and turning over in bed was a major and exhausting undertaking. It looked as if it would snow before the day was out.

Perhaps it was the threat of a storm that set her to thinking about Alexander. It was a day very similar to the one on which she had first met him. She could not shake off her thoughts of him, though she tried to keep herself busy as far as the advanced condition of her pregnancy would allow. She sat finally in the morning room putting the finishing touches to a gorgeously embroidered christening robe that she made for her child. He would come for the christening, of course. Perhaps duty would make him come as soon as she was able to send him the news that his heir had been born.

Alexander. She gazed through the window at the gray world without and saw him as he had appeared to her on that first evening: handsome, vibrant, almost dangerously attractive. He had appeared like a creature from another world. She saw him as he had been at Portland House: disdainful, contemptuous, aloof, yet inexplicably tender and passionate in their more intimate encounters. She returned her attention to her embroidery. She must not allow herself to indulge in memory. Not only was it a pointless exercise, but some instinct of self-defense warned her that her fragile peace of mind could be shattered very easily if she did not cling to the present and the immediate future.

It was at this moment that the she felt the first of the pains, a stabbing sensation and a tightening of muscles that robbed her of breath for a moment and left her feeling frightened and very much alone. She continued to embroider, every nerve in her body tensed for another sign that her time had indeed come. When she had counted eight such pains, she rang for Mrs. Rush and calmly suggested that the doctor be summoned. A half-hour later she was in

bed, knowing that the pains were not going to stop.
She wanted Alexander.

The doctor, standing at a window gazing out into
the darkness, turned as the bedroom door opened,
and his eyes widened in surprise. He took one step
in its direction but stopped when he saw Mrs. Rush
about the same errand, horror written large on her
face.

"My lord," she said in an urgent whisper, "this is
no place for you. Do go downstairs at once and I
shall have Dodd bring you refreshment. I shall come
myself to inform you as soon as there is any news."

Merrick brushed past her just as if she were not
there. His face was still deathly pale. He stood looking at the bed, where his wife lay on her side facing
away from him, breathing in deep gasps, whose du-
ration she seemed to be trying to control. She moaned
quietly to herself before relaxing and turning her
face into the pillow.

Mrs. Rush hesitated for a moment, threw a hasty
and pleading glance in the direction of the viscount,
and bustled to the bed, where she dipped a cloth
into a basin of water and proceeded to dab at her
mistress's hot face.

Merrick continued to stand just inside the door,
which he had closed behind him. He watched Anne
for a couple of minutes until the pain gripped her
again and her breathing again became deep and
even in her attempt to control panic. He watched, as
he had when he had first entered the room, one
hand come behind her back and push ineffectually
against her lower back. He did not remove his eyes
even when the doctor crossed the room to his side.

"My lord," that flustered individual said in a lowered voice, "I really must ask that you leave the
room now. It is not at all fitting for you to be here.
There is really nothing to be done at the moment. I
must wait until her ladyship is ready to deliver. I
assure you that all is well under control, and Mrs.

Rush is an able assistant. But there is no knowing how long it will be."

Merrick did not reply. So this was what he had brought her to. He had forced her against her will to cater to his pleasure, and now he must watch her suffering cruelly to deliver a child she had never desired. He would not leave. If she must suffer, the least he could do was to stay with her and know the full extent of his guilt. He looked at her hair, damp and tumbled around her face and over the pillow, and at the one flushed cheek that he could see. He looked at her swollen form clearly outlined against the sheet that was her sole covering. When she tensed again against pain, he strode across to the bed, gently removed the hand that had come to support her back again, and placed his own palms against her back, pressing firmly and slowly massaging.

"Oh, thank you, Mrs. Rush," she said faintly when the pain had once more receded. Her eyes were closed and she had turned her face again into the pillow. "That felt very good."

Mrs. Rush, flushed with embarrassment, glared uneasily across the bed at her employer.

It seemed as if it would never end. She had stopped an hour or more ago asking the doctor when she might expect it to be all over. His answers had been so soothingly noncommittal that she had realized that he did not know any more than she how much longer she must endure this labor. She was in a haze of pain and exhaustion, willing herself to relax and rest in the intervals between pain, which were becoming shorter and shorter, and steeling herself to endure without panic the pains, which were becoming more severe. If they continued much longer, she felt, she must give in to the urge to scream and fight in order to be free of the crashing pains, which were very nearly beyond her endurance.

The hands at her back helped. They were strong and warm and somehow braced her against the terrible force that seemed to be tearing her spine in two.

She pushed herself against them and concentrated on the comfort they brought, a comfort that was not only physical. In a strange way those hands also cushioned her against the loneliness of her labor. They became disembodied in her tired mind. Although one part of her brain assumed that they belonged to Mrs. Rush, it did not occur to her to find it strange that that lady was in front of her each time the pains subsided to smooth back the hair from her flushed face and to sponge her face and neck with cool water.

"Doctor Selby," Anne cried finally, panic in her voice. She surged over onto her back. "I cannot . . . I must . . . I have to push!" And she immediately suited action to words, bearing down against her pain in nature's effort to rid herself of her burden.

Both the doctor and Mrs. Rush jumped into action, but the latter did not neglect to glare meaningfully at Merrick and order him from the room, almost as if she were the employer and he the servant. Anne turned her head, her pain for the moment in abeyance, and looked without surprise into her husband's eyes. Of course! She would have known it was he if only her mind had not been dulled by exhaustion. As she felt again the tightening sensation that was now such a familiar warning of pain to come, she reached for his hands at the same moment as they came out to her. They gripped each other, one set of hands on either side of her head while the doctor positioned her for birth and while their daughter made a hurried entry into the world.

Viscount Merrick left his wife's bedchamber ten minutes later, when it appeared likely to him that she would survive her ordeal and that the child was safely launched into life. They had not spoken. She had taken the red and wrinkled little bundle of humanity that was their daughter and put it to her breast, and she had gazed up at him, her face still flushed, her eyes bright and anxious. Was she still so afraid of him? Did she think that he still meant her harm?

He had gazed back at her unsmilingly and finally lowered his eyes to the child. His daughter. Their daughter. The product of lust on the one hand and duty on the other? No, he would not believe so. Whenever the child had been conceived, she was a product of love on his part. His love for her mother had been growing steadily through those two weeks of the spring, even if he had not admitted it to himself until the end. Although the child was far from beautiful in her newly born state, Merrick felt a rush of love for her. His daughter, whom Anne had carried and borne. He would take her home with him so that his wife might be free to forget his past cruelties and his very existence if she wished. And he would devote the coming years to the upbringing of his child, Anne's child.

When Merrick had returned his gaze to his wife's face, she had been lying with her eyes closed. He had turned and quietly left the room.

15 Anne did not see a great deal of her husband during the following few days, while she lay in bed, strictly forbidden by the doctor to get up, though she chafed to do so. Merrick visited her twice each day, always for a few minutes only. Each time he asked about her health and made labored conversation before turning to the cradle beside her bed where Lady Catherine Mary Stewart lay, placidly oblivious to her impressive name and title. He would stand gazing down at her, rarely touching the child and never picking her up.

Only once in all the visits did Anne see him smile. He had taken the child's hand in his and spread the tiny and perfect fingers across one of his own. He smiled fleetingly as the baby's fingers curled around his. Anne felt grateful relief. Perhaps his apparently morose mood was due more to indifference than to actual hostility to his daughter. He had not expressed disappointment at her failure to present him with a son.

She expected him to leave within a few days and was surprised when he made no mention of doing so. When she was finally on her feet again, the reason became apparent. The garden that spread from beneath her window was blanketed with several inches

of snow. It looked thick enough to make it likely that
the roads were near impassable. But she discovered
another reason the same day, when she was sitting
opposite her husband at the long dining-room table.
It was the first time they had sat thus since their
wedding night, and she wondered if the same thoughts
and memories were plaguing his mind. Apparently not.

"We will have to postpone Catherine's christening
for at least a month," Merrick said abruptly, breaking a long silence. "It will be impossible for anyone
to travel for at least another few weeks."

"You mean the vicar?" Anne asked in surprise.

"I mean Grandmamma and Grandpapa," he replied. "And I know that Freddie and Ruby wish to
come, and I believe some of the others too. I have not
heard from your brother yet. I do not know what his
intentions will be."

"Bruce?" Anne asked. "You have written to him?"

"Of course," Merrick said. "The birth of a daughter is an important event in our lives, is it not?"

"And Grandmamma is coming? Here?"

Merrick's face relaxed into a smile. "I believe she
will," he said. "A reply came to my announcement
this morning, quite a prompt response, considering
the state of the roads. Grandmamma announced that
we were to go there for the christening as everyone
always has for any major family event. But on this
occasion I plan to remain firm. My own home is the
most fitting setting for the christening of our first
child. Especially now, Anne. What have you done
with the place? It is almost unrecognizable."

"You said I might do as I wished here," Anne said
anxiously, "and I have kept expenses to a minimum.
In many instances it was just a case of moving things
and displaying them to greater advantage. Do you
dislike any of the changes?"

"Not one," he said with conviction. "You have
changed Redlands from a house to a home, Anne.
And the gardener keeps telling me with an air of
great mystery and importance that I should just wait

until the spring comes and I can see what you have done with the gardens. It seems I have no choice but to do so."

"I do hope you like it," Anne said. "It really looks at its best in the spring when the daffodils are in bloom against the house as well as the bluebells and primroses in the woods. But the formal gardens are my pride and joy. It is with them that I began the changes to Redlands."

"Do you like it here?" Merrick asked, real curiosity in his voice.

"It is home," she replied. "I cannot imagine living anywhere else."

The silence that ensued was not an uncomfortable one. Each was pondering what the other had said. Merrick was amazed to find his wife apparently placid, seemingly contented with her lot. Seeing the house as it was now, completely transformed from the rather shabby gloom that he had always associated with the place, he was not completely surprised that she found it a pleasant home, but her manner seemed to go beyond mere acceptance. He did not find the bitter unhappiness and accusatory glances that he had fully expected. If he could but take the child away from her and allow her to resume the life that she had somehow contrived to make meaningful, perhaps at some time in the future he would be able to forgive himself for his past treatment of her. Perhaps his feelings of guilt would finally go away.

Anne's mind was humming. He was going to stay for at least a month or perhaps longer. He had just spoken as if he were planning to see the garden in the spring. For a few weeks they would be almost like a family. So far there had been none of the impatience and contempt in his manner that she had seen during several of their previous encounters. There was an aloofness, a lack of humor, perhaps, but she would endure that for the sake of future memories. If she could but contrive not to anger him, she would be able to remember for the lifetime ahead these few weeks when they had lived here together, the three of them.

Her cheeks burned for a moment and she lowered her head over her plate as she remembered that Alexander had been with her through much of her labor and through the whole of her delivery. It had seemed so natural at the time to turn and see him there, to cling to him during those agonizing minutes while she gave birth. But why had he done it? It was unheard of for a husband even to enter his wife's room during the process of childbirth. But to stay there and witness all! What must the servants think?

Grandmamma was coming and even Grandpapa. Alexander seemed convinced that they would do so, though for years they had hardly ventured beyond the confines of their estate, except for an occasional visit to London, and he had invited the other members of the family too and her brother and sister-in-law. It was all very bewildering. He was making a big event of the birth of this child, and she was not even a son. She had criticized him for many things, even hated him for a few, but she must be eternally grateful for this. His public recognition of her as his wife and the mother of his child could do her nothing but good in the neighborhood, and his recognition of Catherine would be invaluable for the child. If he was angry with her for not giving him a boy, he had certainly decided to hide his anger. Anne stole a look at her husband down the length of the table and found him contemplating her moodily, a glass of red wine twirling absently between his fingers.

The days and eventually the weeks passed almost pleasantly. There were times when Anne could almost imagine that they were any ordinary family. She did not see much of Alexander. Having never taken any real interest in the running of his estate, he was now making an effort to get to know his own property. He spent long hours behind shut doors in consultation with his estate manager, and the two of them several times waded off through the snow, wearing heavy boots and muffled to the eyes in warm clothes.

But there were times when they were together, and they were on the whole surprisingly pleasant times. He visited the nursery more than once each day, and sometimes Anne was there too. He never touched the child when she was there, but once when she entered the room without warning, he was holding the baby in front of him, one hand cupped beneath her head, smiling into her open but unfocused eyes. The smile remained even when he turned to see Anne in the doorway.

"She has my hair," he said, "but she is going to have your heart-shaped face. Look at her pointed chin."

And Anne moved to his side and looked with him at the child. Their arms almost touched. Catherine herself broke the magic of that moment by suddenly flapping her little arms as if she thought she was about to be dropped and beginning to cry. Merrick handed her immediately to Anne, and after watching in silence for a minute or two while she rocked and soothed the baby against her shoulder, he left the room.

They always had dinner together, sitting a ridiculously long distance from each other at either end of the dining table. And they always made conversation somehow. They talked about the house and the grounds, about the baby, about his family. He told her about London, about the Prince Regent and the royal family, about the more entertaining tidbits of gossip. It was on these topics that the conversation sometimes died. It seemed that he suddenly remembered that he lived there apart from her, that he had fled there to escape her at the start of their marriage.

After almost a month of snow and cold weather that kept it on the ground, conditions finally changed and the snow began to melt. For more than a week longer the roads were even more difficult to travel

than they had been while the cold spell remained.
But eventually the ground started to dry, and then
visitors began to come to pay their respects to the
viscount, who was very rarely seen in the neighborhood, and to congratulate Anne on the birth of the
child. Merrick never avoided these visitors, but seemed
almost to enjoy their presence. He always treated
Anne with the utmost courtesy and always rang himself to summon the nurse and the baby.

Anne was sorry to see the snow disappear. Now it
would be possible for the family members to travel
to the christening, and there would be no further
cause for delay. Alexander, in fact, set the date one
evening while they were at dinner, for a day in the
second half of February. It was less than two weeks
away. Once that was over, there would be nothing
else to keep him there. He would return to his life in
London and she might never see him again. She had
made the choice the previous year to live apart from
him, but now she sometimes wished that she could
be given the choice again. It was true that they did not
have anything like a close relationship, but the hostility
seemed to have disappeared, and it was pleasant to
know that she would see him perhaps several times
in the course of a day and that they would dine together each night. It would be harder than ever now
to be alone again after having spent these weeks
with him.

In the meanwhile, there was the christening to
prepare for and several guests to cater to. The duke
and duchess were indeed coming, and Freddie and
Ruby. Alexander had asked her if she would approve of asking the latter couple to be their daughter's godparents. Stanley and Celia were coming too,
without their children. And Jack, inexplicably, had
dashed off a brief acceptance of the invitation. Most
surprising of all, Anne felt, was the fact that her
brother and his wife were also coming. It would be
the first time she had seen Bruce since her wedding
day. It was an exciting time, but the pleasure was

always offset by the knowledge that the sooner the event came, the sooner she would lose her husband.

Freddie and Ruby were the first to arrive, the day before they were expected.

"Frederick wished to set out two days ago," Ruby explained to Anne in her rather strident manner when the two were alone. "He was terrified that we would have an accident with the carriage or that the horses would become lame on a lonely country road or that we might have a spring snowstorm or that somehow Alexander had mistaken the date of the christening in the letter he sent us. I persuaded him to wait until today, but it would have been too distressing for him to have to wait until tomorrow. I hope we are not inconveniencing you dreadfully, but I guessed that Alexander at least would not be surprised to see us. I believe Frederick has a reputation for arriving early for important events."

"I am quite delighted to see you both," Anne said sincerely, "and, yes, Alexander has warned me that you might be early. He did think that perhaps your influence would have taken away some of Freddie's anxieties." She smiled.

"Oh, some, yes," Ruby agreed. "But I have no intention of taking over Frederick's life altogether, you know. I am aware that many people think that he is not too well-endowed with brains, and I am perfectly well aware that many people think I married him only because of his position and wealth, but I do not care. Frederick is a precious individual, for all people say, and I am quite willing to put up with his eccentricities and his abominable taste in dress in exchange for his great good nature and kindness." Ruby looked at Anne penetratingly, as if daring her to offer a contradictory opinion.

Anne clasped her hands against her breasts. She did consider hugging Ruby but had second thoughts. Somehow Freddie's wife did not seem quite the kind of woman one hugged impulsively. "Oh, I am so glad," she said. "I love Freddie very dearly and was afraid that he would not get what he deserves in life. I am so pleased that you married him, Ruby."

They found the subject of their conversation in the nursery with Merrick, dangling the baby in front of his face and giggling into her wide, toothless smile.

"She likes me," he said.

"The child is too young to smile. She has wind, Frederick," Ruby informed him bluntly.

"I think perhaps it is your waistcoat that is catching her eye," Merrick said, leaning against the mantel and viewing his cousin and his daughter with an amused eye. "Where did you find that particular shade of orange, Freddie? I'll wager it glows in the dark. Never tell me Weston made it for you."

"Frederick does not even patronize him anymore," Ruby said, advancing into the room and apparently doing a mental estimate of the baby's safety. "If the silly man does not want our custom, then we will take it elsewhere. And that is what we do, is it not, my love?"

Freddie lowered the baby and smiled fondly at his mate. "Ruby told me to set my own fashions if I wish," he said. "She has faith in me. Brains. Ruby has brains like you, Alex. I'm a lucky man to have her. Like you with Anne."

"Yes," Merrick said, his eyes straying to his wife.

Jack arrived before luncheon the following day. He had stayed overnight with friends who lived a mere twelve miles away, he explained. After luncheon he suggested that Anne take a stroll in the garden with him.

"I say," he said when she took him onto the graveled walks among the geometrically arranged box hedges, lawns, flower gardens, and fountain, "what has happened here? The last time I came the whole place looked hopelessly overgrown and dreary. Did you do this, Anne?"

"Yes, I did," she said. "Of course, you are not seeing it nearly at its best. The spring flowers should be blooming within the next few weeks. That is my favorite time."

"Ah," said Jack, leaning toward her and drawing her hand through his arm, "do I read an invitation in those words, Anne?"

She laughed. "Do you never give up, Jack? Would you even know how to talk to a woman without flirting with her, I wonder?"

"I have never felt the urge to flirt with Grand-mamma," he said.

Anne laughed again. "I should love you to see the garden in the spring," she said. "If you also wish to do so, you must wangle an invitation from Alexander."

"I must confess," he said, "that this relationship of yours definitely intrigues me. I admitted defeat last spring only because I thought you two were patching up your differences. Then you left alone, and Alex was not worth talking to for the day before the rest of us left. Then I heard through a circuitous route that you were with child. And now Alex has been here for weeks. So what, Anne? Are you finally together, you two?"

"We are married whether we live together or not, Jack," Anne said evasively. "So you must start treating me like a cousin, if you please, instead of one of your flirts."

Jack sighed. "Do you at least have some neighbors with unmarried daughters?" he asked.

Anne laughed.

Bruce's wife was a surprise. Anne had not met her before. She had expected a plain and practical girl, rather like Freddie's Ruby, perhaps. Ethel was, in fact, a tiny and very pretty girl with masses of dark hair and large eyes to match. She did not say very much, and Anne gathered from the little she did say that she was not overintelligent. But she was a re-markably good-natured girl and smiled a great deal. She appeared to worship Bruce and gazed askance at anyone who opposed his opinions.

She seemed awed by the superior company in which

they found themselves, especially after the arrival of the duke and duchess late in the day, and frequently escaped to the nursery to play with Catherine. She confided to Anne, when the latter found her there on one occasion, that she thought herself to be in a delicate condition. But she had not told even Bruce, believing that he would have forbidden her to come if he had known. And she had so looked forward to meeting her sister-in-law and her new niece.

The duke had to be helped into the house by two footmen and complained gruffly about the rigors of travel when winter was hardly over. But he had been in the house barely a half-hour when he insisted on climbing the stairs with the aid of his cane to view his new great-granddaughter. He would not hear of having her brought down to the drawing room.

"Children are too often lugged around and put on view for everyone's admiration," he said, growling to Jack to pass him his cane and puffing to his feet. "If people want to see 'em, they should be the ones to do the traveling."

But when he came back downstairs, the duchess was at his side, Catherine in her arms.

"She was crying," Her Grace said, "and Nurse insisted that there was nothing wrong except that the child has had too much excitement and too many visitors in the last day or two. But I could not leave the little mite like that. See what you can do with her, Anne, dear."

But it was Merrick who reached for the baby and soothed her against his shoulder as the child sucked loudly on a mouthful of his neckcloth. The duchess looked from him to Anne, who was pouring tea, nodded briskly, looked significantly at her husband, and helped herself to a scone.

"Let someone revive the conversation in this room quickly," Jack said languidly, lowering his teacup to the saucer, "or Grandmamma will be suggesting that we prepare some theatricals for the christening party. I assume you have arranged such an occasion, Alex?"

The next few days were busy ones for Anne, who was unused to entertaining in her own home. They were happy days. She felt thoroughly part of Alexander's family and had passed the stage of being either cowed by the duchess's brisk manner or awed by the duke's surface gruffness. She felt unexpected delight in conversing with her brother now that her days were no longer ruled by his gloomy outlook on life.

She was excited by the day of the christening and by the extra entertaining that had been organized for the occasion. Lady Catherine Stewart behaved herself in a manner very nearly fitting to her station. Waving arms and feet succeeded in bunching the gorgeous christening robe around her waist on more than one occasion, and she beamed toothlessly—all except a skeptical Ruby insisted that it was her first real smile—when the vicar poured water over her head instead of maintaining an expression of cool disdain. But she did not cry or disgrace herself in any other way.

Only one cloud hung over those days as far as Anne was concerned. All the guests were to leave three days after the christening. And then there would be nothing to keep Alexander at home. On the following day, or very soon afterward, she was convinced, he too would leave and she would be left to try somehow to make something meaningful of the years ahead with Catherine. She would have the rare letter from him probably, and doubtless she would hear news of him occasionally from people like Sonia, who still resided in London. But it was not likely to be the kind of news that she would welcome. The name of his newest mistress, perhaps. So she clung to these final days greedily, willing time to go slowly.

By teatime on the third day following the christening, they were alone again at Redlands, the three of them.

16 A whole week had passed since the departure of their last guest after the christening. Merrick was well aware that he was outstaying his welcome, that he was not being fair to Anne. Redlands was the only place she could call home, and she had spent a great deal of time and creativity on making it a pleasant environment. She had made it clear to him a year ago that she wished to live there, and that she did not wish to live with him. He owed it to her to leave her alone there, and he really had no excuse for further delay. He must leave within the next few days.

But it was so hard to make the break. Even though they had not had a close relationship since his arrival from London, there had been a certain harmony between them. There had certainly not been any unpleasantness, and at times he had almost been lulled into the delusion that they were any ordinary family, delighting in an attractive home, in each other's presence, and in the pleasure of a new child. But he must not forget that it was not really true. It was not fair to Anne for him to go on fooling himself any longer.

He did not know quite what he was going to do when he returned to London. His not-insubstantial

mansion in the city would seem bleak and empty
without Anne, and the activities that life there offered would appear even more shallow and mean-
ingless than they had in the last year. He had never
wanted to live in the country since leaving his grandparents' home to go to school. He had always thought
that life had nothing duller to offer. Now he would
have liked nothing more than to settle down to a
quiet domestic life with his wife and daughter.

His daughter. At least he would have Catherine to
give some meaning to his life and to remind him of
Anne. She was a thorough delight. As soon as he
returned home, he must find her a suitable nurse.
But he did not intend abandoning her to the care of
servants. He was going to be an attentive father. It
was ironic, really, that he had never been fond of
children. He had never noticed them, in fact. Yet
now he was contemplating the care of his daughter
as the brightest spot in his future.

Merrick was standing in the library, a glass of
brandy in his hand, staring out into the darkness of
late evening. Calling the room a library, he thought,
turning to look around him, was to dignify the room
considerably. There were very few books there. Now
if he were to move here from London, he could
bring his substantial library with him. His books would
show to advantage in this room, which Anne had
brightened with new green velvet drapery, an Orien-
tal rug, and a newly varnished desk. He would be
able to sit there, in that old leather chair before the
fire, reading, knowing that at any time he could put
down the book and join his wife in another room of
the house.

Merrick made a gesture of impatience and drank
the remains of his brandy in one gulp. There was no
point in such self-indulgent thoughts. That was his
trouble. He had always been insufferably selfish. Let
him do one selfless deed in his life. No more talking
about leaving. He would do it the next day. He
would go now and tell Anne. She might as well know

as soon as possible that the peace was to be restored to her life before another day had passed. She should know that soon all traces of his presence would be removed from her life. He put his glass down on the desk and strode from the room.

Anne was in her own room, ready for bed. She had put on her nightgown and brushed out her hair. Bella had been dismissed for the night. The baby had been fed. It was so much easier now that she was sleeping through the night. She was standing by the window of her room, staring out into the darkness. It was almost March, almost spring. She had smelled it in the air that morning, when she had been walking in the garden. Soon the first flowers would be in bloom. Would Alexander see them? Somehow it seemed very important to her that he should. Almost she felt she would be safe if he could only see the spring blooms, though she could not explain to herself why she felt this way. It was no good, though. She must reconcile herself to the fact that he would go soon. She could not keep him much longer.

There was a brief tap on her door and it opened. Anne turned, expecting to see Bella returned for some forgotten item. Her eyes widened when her husband stepped into the room.

"My apologies," he said. "I did not realize that you had retired already. But I did not wish to wait until morning. I shall be leaving tomorrow, Anne."

Her stomach lurched and her knees felt weak, but she showed no outward sign. "I see," she said.

"You will be glad to see me go," he said abruptly. "Soon your garden will be keeping you busy, I expect."

"Yes," she said.

"I shall try to leave before noon," he said, "so that we can be home before dark. I shall take the carriage and have it returned within a few days for your convenience."

"Yes," Anne said, "that sounds sensible." Her hands were twisting the sides of her nightgown.

"I shall take Nurse with me and hire a wet-nurse as soon as we reach London," he said.

"What?"

"Is she too young to be weaned?" he asked. "I am not sure. I have meant to ask you."

"What are you talking about?" Anne was whispering.

"I shall take Catherine with me tomorrow," he said. "Perhaps she is too young to be taken from you, but I thought it best to take her when I am here to care for her and protect her on the way. My God, Anne!"

Merrick lunged forward and caught his wife as her knees buckled under her. He could almost feel sound coming from her before the terrible wail finally escaped her lips.

"My God," he said, "what is it?"

But Anne could only wail and clutch at him. He looked around for a glass of water and cursed the luckless Bella when he found none.

Finally Anne's hysteria gave way to sobs, but she continued to clutch at Merrick's sleeves. "Oh, you could not be so cruel," she managed to get out between sobs. "Don't be so cruel, Alexander. Please. Oh, what have I ever done to deserve this. Oh, please, no. I just want to die."

Merrick took her firmly by the arms and sat her down on the edge of the high bed. He knelt on the floor in front of her and smoothed a damp strand of hair away from her face. "What is it?" he said. "What have I done?"

Anne covered her face with her hands. "Don't take Catherine from me, Alex," she said, still unable to control her sobs. "Please, anything but that. Don't take her from me. She is all I have."

He stared up at her for a moment and then got to his feet and drew her into his arms, pressing her face against his shoulder. "Anne," he said against her hair, "I didn't know. Don't distress yourself like this. I didn't know."

She was too distraught to hear him. "Please, Alex,"

she said. "Please. Don't take Catherine. Oh, I shall
die. I shall die." She put her arms up around his
neck and clung to him.

"Hush," he said, rocking her in his arms. "Hush,
love. I would not hurt you for worlds. Hush now."

Anne still did not hear his words. But some in-
stinctive part of herself knew that there was comfort
somewhere within reach. She turned a tearstained
face up to him without even knowing she did so,
without even seeing him. And he kissed her.

They were both shaken, Anne by the terrible shock
of knowing that he meant to take her daughter away
from her, he by the realization that he would not
even have the child with whom to comfort himself
when he left the following day. Grief on both sides
quickly ignited into passion. They set each other on
fire with eager, searching hands, hot, demanding
mouths and tongues, and bodies that arched into
each other. They reached blindly for the ultimate
comfort, the ultimate release from feelings that were
too intense to be borne.

Merrick tore at her nightgown, too impatient to
open the buttons down the front, and lifted her
naked body onto the bed. He followed her there in
but a few moments, his own clothes having suffered
just as rough a fate. He came between her thighs
and pushed urgently into her so that she cried out
and twined her arms and legs around him. And
together they found a rhythm intense in its need to
be completed. He thrust deeper and deeper into
her, and she opened and lifted herself more intimately against him, each straining for the unity that
their love craved, both believing in their hearts that
it was in reality but a one-sided experience. Yet they
reached their climax together and murmured their
release against each other's lips.

When rational thought returned, Anne found herself lying in the crook of her husband's arm, both of
them still warm and damp from the exertions of

their passion, covered by a disordered tumble of blankets, which Alexander must have pulled over them. She felt sore. It was almost a year since he had last used her, and she supposed that recent childbirth had left her tender. It would pass. It was almost a pleasant discomfort, caused as it was by the body of her husband, whom she loved. She turned further into the warmth of the naked man beside her.

Childbirth! Her eyes opened wide and she jerked away from him so that she might look into his face. He was looking back at her, a strange, almost bitter twist to his mouth.

"You are going to take Catherine from me," she accused. "You cannot do it, Alexander. I shall fight you. I promise I shall fight you. She is my daughter. I carried her for more then eight months and I suffered to bring her into the world. She needs me. I still have the milk that feeds her. And I shall not allow you to take her from me. You have always been a taker, have you not? You have taken from me all I have to give except my daughter. I will not allow you to take her. I won't allow it, Alexander. Please, oh, please, don't take her from me."

Her head still rested against his arm; her hand was still splayed across his warm chest. His mouth tightened into a parody of a smile.

"Don't distress yourself, ma'am," he said quietly. "I have done all the taking from you that I intend to do. I shall complete the process tomorrow by taking myself permanently from your presence. My apologies for tonight. I did not intend for this to happen. And you can set your mind at rest about our daughter. She will remain with you here. I will not take her from you. She is more yours than mine. I merely begot her in a moment of pleasure. You have suffered for her."

He eased his arm from beneath her head and swung himself out of the bed. He dressed quickly and left the room.

* * *

The moring was almost over. He should have been on his way before now. Even if he left within the next quarter of an hour, he would have to ride hard to arrive home before dark. He would not, of course, take the carriage now. There was little point when he would be traveling alone. His belongings could be sent on after him, as they had when he came. There was no purpose in his delaying any longer. He had told Dodd at breakfast that he would not be at home for luncheon.

Merrick wandered on, leaving Anne's formal garden and strolling to the line of trees that bordered it on the west. The sun was shining from a cloudless sky. The air was almost warm. It was easy now to believe that spring was coming. Soon the garden behind him would be a blaze of color. And he would not see it. Anne would wander there, picking daffodils. The baby would see it. Probably by summer she would be crawling over the lawns, and Anne and the gardener would be constantly running after her to prevent her from plucking the heads off the flowers. But he would not see her.

Something caught his eye in the greening grass among the trees. It looked like a frail relic of the winter that had passed. He stooped down and looked with delight at the first flower of spring. He touched it gently with one finger.

Anne had walked out into the garden. She shivered slightly, but it was not really cold, she thought, raising her face to the sun. There was warmth today, and it was pleasant to be out of doors, despite the fact that she had neither cloak nor bonnet. She did not intend to be outside for long. She did not wish to miss Alexander when he left. She had been in the nursery all morning, playing with Catherine. She meant to bring her outside following her afternoon sleep, but this morning she had stayed indoors, expecting every moment that he would come to bi them farewell. She knew he had not left yet. His greatcoat and hat were still in the hall.

It would have been better really if he had slipped away during the morning without a word to anyone. This waiting was killing her. She would see him one more time, probably for a few brief moments only. She would have to pack a lifetime of looking and listening into those moments.

"Anne."

She looked back to the house, though the voice had not come from that direction.

"Anne," he said again, and she saw that he was among the trees, stooping down in the long grass.

She walked toward him consciously drinking in the sight of him, his thick dark hair blown rather untidily around his face, his handsome features turned toward her, his broad shoulders filling out the fine blue broadcloth of his coat. She wanted to smile, but her face felt stiff with the tension she was feeling.

"Come and look at this," he said, and he turned back to look into the grass.

Anne stepped closer and then she sank to her knees on the grass beside him, her face suddenly and unconsciously smiling. "Oh, it is a snowdrop," she said. "The first one, Alex. Spring is here." She reached out and cupped the tiny bloom in her hands. "Look. It has all the beauty of nature in it."

Merrick watched her as she gazed, rapt, at the tiny flower. He ached to touch her, to tell her that he loved her, to beg her to take him back, give him another chance. But he had renounced selfishness where she was concerned. He had told her the night before that he was done with taking from her. And he had spent a sleepless night castigating himself for what he had done to her earlier. To have forced her yet again to accept his attentions, to have put her yet again in danger of having to bear a child of his was unpardonable. Why was it that he always had behaved at his worst with Anne, with the woman whom he loved more dearly than he could ever have imagined loving anyone? He stood up.

"I shall be going, Anne," he said.

She gazed up at him blankly, her hands still cupping the snowdrop. "Oh," she said, and she stood up slowly.

They gazed at each other in silence for a few moments. Merrick held out his right hand. "Will you shake my hand, Anne?" he asked quietly. "Can we part on friendly terms? Do you think you will be able to think kindly of me after I have gone?"

Anne stared at his hand for a long while before she put her own into it. She did not answer him or look up at him. She looked at their clasped hands. Only when, finally, he moved to raise her hand to his lips did she tear it away and look up into his eyes, her own full of agony. She threw her arms up around his neck and buried her face against the folds of his neckcloth.

"Alex," she said.

His arms went tightly around her and he hugged her to him. But he did not say anything. He was stunned.

"Alex," she said, and she lifted her head and looked up into his face, panic spread all over her own. "Don't go. Don't leave me. Stay here with us. Catherine needs you. Or let us come with you. You said last year that I might come. I would not be any trouble to you, I swear I would not. You may live exactly as you please. You need not know I am there. But just so that I may see you, Alex, and know something of your life. And so that Catherine may grow up with a papa. I will not interfere with your pleasures. You may come and go as you please. I shall not even complain about your m-mistresses. And you need not take me about if you would rather not. I shall be contented to stay at home. And at night I can please you. I do please you, then, do I not, Alex? I know I do. Perhaps I can bear you an heir. That would please you too, would it not?"

She had to stop. Her sobs were making it difficult to get the words past her lips. And, indeed, she did not know what she had said. His hands gripping tightly the sides of her head made it difficult for her to hear her own words.

"Anne," he was saying. "Anne, what are you telling me? What are you saying, love?"

She could not even see him clearly. Her tears were making him blur before her sight. She blinked her eyes in annoyance. But with her clearing sight came the realization of what she had done. She put her hands over his and tried to ease them away from the sides of her head.

"I am sorry," she said, and she could feel her face flushing hotly. "I am sorry, Alexander. I did not sleep well last night, and I always hate saying goodbye to people. Forgive me, please. I am delaying you. Let us return to the house."

"Not until you have told me what you meant just now," Merrick said. He resisted the pull of her fingers and still held her head firmly cupped in his hands. She was not allowed to look away. "Why do you wish to live with me? I thought you could hardly wait for the day when I would be gone out of your life forever."

Her cheeks still felt hot. "I am tired," she said. "I am not myself, Alexander. Please forget what I said. They were very foolish words."

"Tell me now," he said quietly, "while you are still looking at me, that you did not mean a word of what you said, that you wish me to go out of your life now within the next few minutes."

She looked silently back into his eyes until his face blurred again. "Let me go, Alex," she said.

"Tell me."

"I cannot," she said. "I cannot say what you wish to hear. I do want to be with you. But you must not fear that I shall forever be begging you to bring me to London. Once you are gone, I shall be strong again. You can be free of me, Alex."

"And if I tell you that I do not wish to be free of you?" he asked.

If only she could see his face clearly! "No," she said, "you must not feel any obligation to me. I know that you married me against your will. I know that I am plain and dull and that I do not fit in with your way of life. I shall be happy here, and I shall have Catherine."

"But Catherine needs a papa," he reminded her. Somehow his forehead was resting against hers.

"Yes," she said lamely.

"Anne," he said softly, "I love you."

Her hands came shakily up to the buttons of his waistcoat, which she began methodically to undo. "No," she said. "Don't do this, Alex. It is sometimes cruel to try to be kind. Go now. Just leave me here and go. Please." She started to do the buttons up again.

"I love you, Anne," he said.

"No, you don't," she said, and realizing that she was about to undo his waistcoat buttons yet again, she splayed her hands across his chest.

"Now, that I cannot accept," he said, and his hands finally came away from her head so that he could put his arms around her and draw her body against his. "I cannot have you call me a liar, you know."

"But you cannot mean it, Alex," she said, looking up again and searching his eyes with her own, which mercifully had cleared once more. "You cannot love me. I am not the woman you would have chosen."

"I have to admit that that is true, love," he said. "I would not have chosen you, and I would have shown a great deal of foolishness in not doing so. I did not love you when I married you, Anne, and I did not love you when I met you again at Grandpapa's last year. But I grew to love you there and I have loved you ever since. I have not enjoyed London since last spring, and there have been no mistresses, you know I had to come when your time was due. And I have not been able to drag myself away since. The though of leaving you has been breaking my heart. Is it possible that I do not have to do so? I do not deserve such good fortune. Tell me the truth now."

"Oh," Anne wailed, dashing the back of her hand across her eyes, "I cannot see you, Alex. I have been such a watering pot in the last few days."

He laughed, "Is that all you can say in a moment of such high tension?" he asked. "Anne, my whole future happiness depends on what you will say in the next few moments. Do you really wish me to stay, love? Can you bear the thought of being my wife in deed as well as in name?"

"Alex," she said, "I have tried and tried to hate you. Sometimes, when you are not here, I almost succeed for five whole minutes at a time. But almost every hour of every day I have to admit to myself that I have loved you since I first set eyes on you. I am sure that I would live without you if you were to leave now. I mean, I do not suppose I really would die of a broken heart or do anything as romantic as that. But, oh, Alex, I feel as if I would die. I mean, I would not want to live."

He clasped her to him, and her arms went up around his neck again. "Last night," he said, "I loved you every moment."

"And I you."

"And last year," he said. "When I started Catherine in you, I did so with love."

"Oh, Alex," she said, and when she raised her face to his, it was glowing and her eyes sparkling, "yes, of course, that is right. Oh, yes, and all our children will begin in the same way, will they not?"

He laughed against her hair. "Yes, love, all of them," he agreed. "But let us put off the delight of planning them all, for the present, anyway. For now I merely want the novelty of making love with you when we both know ourselves loved. Shall we?"

"Oh, yes," she said, smiling up at him.

"Soon?"

"Yes, Alex."

"Now?"

"I think Dodd would be scandalized if we both disappeared upstairs so close to luncheon time," Anne said.

"Let's scandalize Dodd, shall we?" he suggested.

"Yes, Alex."

He hugged her to him again and rocked her against him. Then he lowered his head to hers and kissed her deeply, fondling her with his hands in a way that would indeed have scandalized Dodd and the whole household staff if they had seen.

Then they turned and, with arms twined around each other's waists, set off in the direction of the house.

The tiny snowdrop, the first, frail promise of spring, bloomed forgotten in the grass behind them.

About the Author

Raised and educated in Wales, Mary Balogh now lives in Saskatchewan, Canada, with her husband Robert and her children Jacqueline, Christopher, and Sian. She is a school principal and an English teacher.